ISBN-13: 978-1998775774

Give feedback on the book at:
lorhainneeckhart@hotmail.com

Twitter: @LEckhart
Facebook: AuthorLorhainneEckhart

Printed in the U.S.A

The Reunion

THE FRIESSENS
BOOK ONE

LORHAINNE ECKHART

The Outsider Series

The Forgotten Child
A Baby And A Wedding
Fallen Hero
The Awakening
Secrets
Runaway
Overdue
The Unexpected Storm
The Wedding

The Friessens: A New Beginning

The Deadline
The Price to Love
A Different Kind of Love
A Vow of Love, A Friessen Family Christmas

The Friessens

The Reunion
The Bloodline
The Promise
The Business Plan
The Decision
First Love
Family First
Leave the Light On
In the Moment
In the Family: A Friessen Family Christmas
In the Silence
In the Stars
In the Charm
Unexpected Consequences
It Was Always You
The First Time I Saw You
Welcome to My Arms
Welcome to Boston (A Paige & Morgan Short Story)
I'll Always Love You
Ground Rules
A Reason to Breathe
You Are My Everything
Anything For You
The Homecoming
Stay Away From My Daughter
The Bad Boy
A Place of Our Own
The Visitor
All About Devon
Long Past Dawn
How to Heal a Heart
Keep Me In Your Heart

The Friessen Family

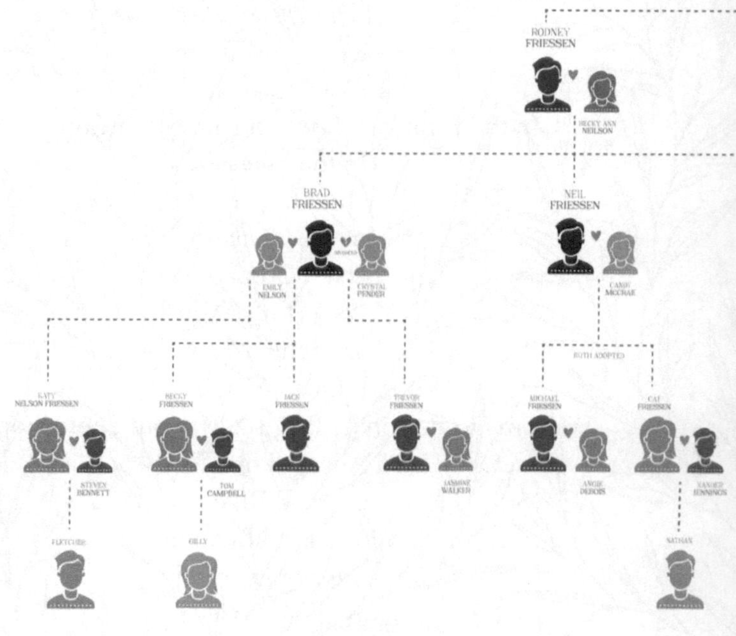

The Outsider Series

THE FORGOTTEN CHILD	BRAD & EMILY
A BABY AND A WEDDING	BRAD & EMILY & and Jed, Neil, Rodney & Becky
FALLEN HERO	JED, DIANA & ANDY
THE SEARCH	JED, DIANA & ANDY
THE AWAKENING	ANDY & LAURA

The Outsider Series

SECRETS	DIANA & JED with the entire Friessen family
RUNAWAY	ANDY & LAURA
OVERDUE	JED & DIANA
THE UNEXPECTED STORM	NEIL & CANDY
THE WEDDING	NEIL & CANDY and the entire Friessen family

The Friessens: A New Beginning

THE DEADLINE	ANDY & LAURA
THE PRICE TO LOVE	NEIL & CANDY
A DIFFERENT KIND OF LOVE	BRAD & EMILY
A VOW OF LOVE	THE ENTIRE
A FRIESSEN FAMILY CHRISTMAS	FRIESSEN FAMILY

The Friessens

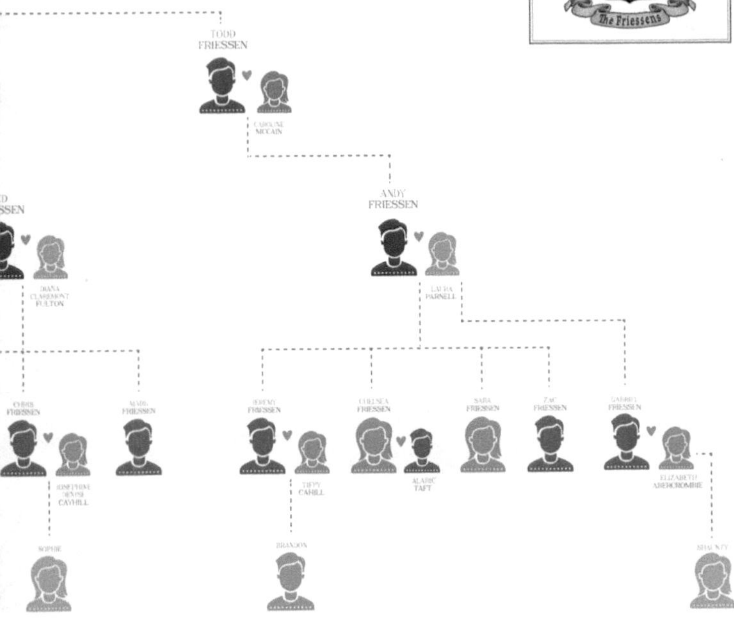

TODD FRIESSEN
CAROLINE MCCAIN
ANDY FRIESSEN
LAURA PARNELL
D...SSEN
DIANA CLAREMONT FULTON
CHRIS FRIESSEN
JOSEPHINE DENISE CAYHILL
MARK FRIESSEN
JEREMY FRIESSEN
TIFFY CAHILL
CHELSEA FRIESSEN
ALARIC TAFT
SARA FRIESSEN
ZAC FRIESSEN
GABRIEL FRIESSEN
ELIZABETH ABERCROMBIE
SOPHIE
BRANDON
BRAELYN

The Friessens

THE ENTIRE FRIESSEN FAMILY
ANDY & LAURA
JED & DIANA
NEIL & CANDY
BRAD & EMILY
KATY & STEVEN
KATY & STEVEN

The Friessens

LEAVE THE LIGHT ON   KATY & STEVEN
IN THE MOMENT   BECKY & TOM
IN THE FAMILY: A Friessen   THE ENTIRE FRIESSEN FAMILY
   Family Christmas
IN THE SILENCE   CAT & XANDER
IN THE STARS   DANNY & EVIE
IN THE CHARM   CHRIS & J.D.
UNEXPECTED CONSEQUENCES   CHRIS & J.D.

The Friessens

IT WAS ALWAYS YOU   KATY & STEVEN
THE FIRST TIME I SAW YOU   GABRIEL & ELIZABETH
WELCOME TO MY ARMS   CHELSEA & ALARIC
WELCOME TO BOSTON   PAIGE & MORGAN
I'LL ALWAYS LOVE YOU   JEREMY
GROUND RULES   JEREMY & TIFFY
A REASON TO BREATHE   TREVOR & JASMINE
YOU ARE MY EVERYTHING   MICHAEL & ANGIE
ANYTHING FOR YOU
THE HOMECOMING   THE ENTIRE FRIESSEN FAMILY

The Reunion

**The family you thought you knew.
A reunion you'll never forget.
A love that lasts forever**

This emotionally charged big family romance will reunite the Friessen family in a heartwarming celebration. Join the entire Friessen family as they all reunite for Becky and Rodney's anniversary. A celebration you won't want to miss.

CHAPTER
One

This wasn't home.

After a moment, when she allowed the confusion to clear, she understood this was where she lived now. It was her new home. She'd survived a stroke, but even through her days of hell, balancing on the edge of leaving this world, she'd never once considered not fighting her way back. She'd lost faith only once in her life, and never again would she believe that taking the easy way out was actually easier. Some days were harder than others, but she pushed on. She couldn't give up.

She'd done that once. That had been a time in her life when she was young and foolish, believing everything she wanted was something she couldn't have. She had always been looking for something better, not understanding that what she already had was all she needed. It was right in front of her, but then, at times she hadn't been able to see it. She had been making choices in fear, acting as if she knew everything. She soon discovered, as the years went by, that she knew nothing at all.

There was a lot to be said for age and wisdom, for

living through every heartbreak imaginable—many of her own making. She hoped she was a better person, all her choices having brought her to this one moment in time. She was Becky Ann Friessen, Rodney's wife, mother to Brad, Neil, and Jed and their wives, Emily, Candy, and Diana. She was a grandmother, a friend.

A breeze picked up, whistling as it stirred the waves over the salty ocean. Becky could hear them pounding the white sandy shore. She could smell the salt in the air, and she breathed again until it settled her. She wanted to go down to the water, to walk there herself and wade into and through the waves as they slapped against her legs, soaking her linen pants. But she wasn't there yet. Almost, she told herself. She believed it as she stared at the cane resting against the light oak nightstand beside the bed, beside the easy chair she was sitting in.

Her skin was damp even with the breeze blowing in. It was warm again, like every other day in Cancun, the home she and Rodney had retired to. She was in the perfect chair before the open window, staring out at the vibrant colors from the gardens below: the reds, greens, oranges, and pinks. Her roses, orchids, and lilies were all in full bloom, and it was in moments like this, when she caught a scent from her garden, that she would remember the young girl who fell in love, had her heart broken, and then pulled a knife across her wrists, allowing the blood to flow out of her just to make the agony stop.

She stared at the white lines now, faded from forty years ago. The memory too had faded over the years—what she had done, what her husband had done. Something happened when you stood between life and death that reminded you of everything you'd forgotten. Becky tried to forget and blank it out as she moved through life, becoming stronger, more confident, and finally feeling as if she was worthy of her husband's love.

She took a breath to clear her head and took in the warm tones of her room, the white trim, and the floor-to-ceiling windows in the pocket doors that could transform the bedroom into a veranda on a whim. This was new, and her son Neil had taken it upon himself to change this bedroom into a paradise while Becky was recovering from her stroke in the rehab center. It was comfortable and nice —and because it was Neil's idea, as always, it was over the top.

She took in the ivy green sectional, the ottoman, and the large flat screen mounted to the wall. She had teased Rodney that their large bed was made for a king, but to her, Rodney was a king, not just for who he was but because he had stayed with her and worked on their marriage, loving her for her.

Rodney wasn't a saint. He was rough around the edges, and he'd made his share of mistakes, her tall, dark-haired, devastatingly handsome man. At times in his younger days, she'd teased him about what a stick in the mud he could be, so set in his ways. He was cocky, arrogant, confident, and there hadn't been a woman around who didn't try to get his attention. He was the son of a wealthy rancher, a senator, a rodeo star. He had been everything to her, as only a young girl with starry eyes could see him.

Rodney had always known what he wanted. Anyone who paid attention could see that. It was in his walk, the way he took in what was going on around him and everyone he was with. He was brilliant. Even at such a young age, as a young man of nineteen, he had known there was more to people than what they said. She didn't know that at the time, but then, everything she'd learned now from her years of struggles allowed her to see how truly special her husband was.

Rodney was the eldest Friessen son. He was a hard worker who made a success out of everything he did: the cattle ranching, his time in the rodeo. He had set eyes on Becky for the first time when they went to the same school, Berkley. She'd heard he was in the rodeo, and she remembered their first date, when she had tagged along with him to the rodeo grounds. He'd ended up facedown in the dirt, scrambling to get out from under a bucking bronco after making his time. He had been amazing.

She remembered it as if it were yesterday. The blueness of his eyes had made her heart skip a beat in her slender chest. Her throat had squeezed at something in his expression that she couldn't put her finger on. His powerful eyes had been set on her. Maybe that was what had made women from everywhere want him. She sure as hell had. He was heart stopping, the best-looking man she'd ever seen, with a body she had wanted to step closer to. The way he moved, his slim hips and long legs…even his deep red checked shirt hadn't been able to hide his chest and shoulders. Rodney Friessen had grabbed her attention.

She'd been sitting on a worn bench, wearing a yellow sundress, watching him. A white sunhat perched on her head, her waist-length hair flowing in soft waves. He glanced her way, then looked once, twice, three times. There was no mistaking it: He'd noticed her. Then he had dug in with each step and walked towards her. It had been a moment in time she'd never forget, burned into her memories. That had been their first date—and the moment she realized she had to have Rodney, that he was the one.

"There you are," her husband's deep voice called out

behind her. "Your nurse is downstairs, ready to go for the day. Are you sure you don't need her to stay?"

She had to blink as her memories flashed from a young, dashing Rodney to her tall, older husband. She swore the man was even more handsome today than he'd been forty-five years earlier. How was it possible for a man to have aged better than a woman? His eyes softened as he stepped closer, resting his large hands on his hips, his gold band flashing on his finger. Then he touched her where she sat in the easy chair, another of Neil's new additions.

Rodney didn't pull away, instead running his large hand over her shoulder and leaning down to kiss her cheek. She pressed her hand over his, maybe to hold him there. She loved his touch and didn't want him to walk away.

"I'm good," she said. The words were coming easier, not as slurred and unclear, but then, she'd fought an aging body and a debilitating stroke that had left her with paralysis on one side. Her mind had remained clear, but she was stuck in a body that didn't want to work. It had been so hard in the beginning, because in her mind, she was still that young, beautiful girl who had stolen Rodney Friessen's heart. Only when she caught a glimpse of the old woman in the mirror staring back at her did the icy reality crash in.

"You sure? This is your first day home." He was worried. She could see it in his expression even though they'd both wanted this for so long.

She patted his hand again and then forced herself to slip to the edge of the chair and push herself up. She reached for the cane as she stood, willing her body to move as she once had. Rodney, of course, didn't let her go but instead held on to her, helping her stand up.

"Don't look so worried. I'm stronger than you think," she said. This was the man she'd married, and she couldn't imagine spending another moment away from him. At the same time, she didn't want him playing nursemaid to her —to see her as useless, frail, and weak. "I wouldn't be home if I couldn't look after myself. You know that. Now why don't you take me downstairs so I can talk to my son about his need to redo our bedroom?"

"You don't like it?" He was still holding on to her, and she loved his touch as a husband, not as a man worried she couldn't keep herself together. "I wanted you to have a space you're comfortable in. I wasn't sure…"

What was he going to say? Was he expecting the nurse he hired to sit up here all day with her? She hoped not. Although she liked Nola, she needed to look after herself. She had struggled to bathe and dress herself for weeks, and she'd be dammed if anyone would treat her like a child incapable of tending to her personal needs. It was degrading, that's what it was. She wouldn't have come home if that were the case. Maybe Rodney needed to understand that.

"Rodney, my love." She reached up and patted his cheek, taking in her wrinkled hand and the dull gold band still on her finger, the same one she'd worn for almost forty-five years from the day Rodney had slipped it on her finger. She didn't think she could get it off now even if she wanted to. "Stop worrying so much. I'm home, and I don't need Nola hovering over me as if I'm going to fall at any moment. This change…" She took in the newly renovated bedroom and the sheer curtains that fluttered when a breeze swept in. "It's lovely. Now let's go."

When she slipped her hand on his arm, he gave her a look as if he didn't quite believe her, but at least this time he started walking with her to the door. His hand latched over hers to hold her to him.

"So tell me, when are all my children arriving?" she

asked. They made it to the top of the stairs, and she focused on the circular stone steps. At one time, she'd loved the deep orange tile, but going up and down these stairs now was better than an aerobics workout at the nearest gym.

"Surprise!"

She nearly dropped her cane at the chorus of voices, looking down into the open foyer where her grown boys, their wives, and her seven grandkids were waiting. "You're here already! Oh, this is wonderful."

One, two, three—she counted them again: Brad, Jed, and Neil with Cat sitting on his shoulders. Her daughter-in-laws, Emily, Diana, and Candy, stood with their husbands, each with an eye on their children, her grandkids. There was something about each one of them, something in their tired, distracted expressions, that Becky recognized all too well. Each woman was holding on to something.

CHAPTER
Two

"Like I told your father, I'm fine. Stop hovering," Becky said. Neil had to be the worst of her children when it came to worrying about her. Not that Brad and Jed hadn't done their share. Her children, her boys, were strong and good looking, just like their father in their own ways, but each as different as the next. At least Neil had started to relax somewhat. She could see this in the way he dressed. He had swapped out the tailored suits he always wore for black cargo shorts today, and his shirt and tie were also gone.

She hadn't seen him dressed up in so long. Even when he'd visited her at rehab, she often saw him in a plain cotton shirt or a simple plain T-shirt. Even his neatly shaven look and short dark hair had changed to a longer style, just brushing his ears, and a five o'clock shadow. It was a look she'd never seen on Neil before. No, it was more like Jed, her youngest, the one who'd insisted on going out on his own and making his own way without any help from his family. He was independent, stubborn. She'd almost lost him.

"I just don't want you to push yourself too hard." He was standing in front of her, looking down on her, his hands on his slim hips.

Becky sat in the easy chair, the leather rustling when she moved. The living room was impressive. She'd almost forgotten how much she loved this room, with its high ceiling, stone fireplace, shades of brown that were almost orange, windows that filled it with light, and the plants that gave it so much life. She squeezed her cane and rested it against the oak side table, the corners of which she suddenly realized weren't suitable for her grandkids.

"Mom, did you hear me?" Neil was still there, and Becky took a breath and glanced up at him.

"Sit down, Neil. I'm not deaf. I'm wondering if you've considered replacing the tables in here."

He seemed at a loss as he stared at her, taking a slow, measured look around as if he couldn't understand what she was talking about.

"Your mom is talking about baby proofing, Neil." Candy, his wife, had perfect curves and gorgeous long dark hair. She, too, was barefoot, wearing black shorts and a floral tank top as she carried their six-month-old baby boy, Michael, who would be crawling soon—and then pulling himself up on the coffee table and falling against one of those sharp corners... No, those tables had to go.

"Baby proofing, why do we need to worry about that now?" Neil leaned down and kissed Candy as she passed him Michael, who was kicking his legs and giggling. Neil raised him above his head and gave him a noisy kiss on his cheek before cuddling him. Becky could see how Neil's son was kicking his legs, bouncing on his hip. Michael would probably be walking before he was a year old.

"How are you feeling, Becky? Can I get you anything?" Candy leaned down and rubbed her arm. Her soft brown eyes were filled with blooming confidence. It seemed, as the days passed, that the terrified young woman who didn't know how to fit in to their world or be Neil's wife was coming into herself.

"You don't need to wait on me, either, Candy. Where is everyone?" She could hear voices coming from the kitchen and others maybe from outside. It seemed quiet in here with just Neil and Candy. She noticed the exchanged glance between husband and wife. Obviously, something was going on.

"Everyone is out back, and I don't mind waiting on you," Candy said. "This is your first time home since the stroke. We just don't want you to overdo it or to be overwhelmed." She glanced at Neil again.

Becky knew something had been discussed, and someone needed to fill her in. "Overwhelmed? Good grief. How could I be overwhelmed being home and with my family? I'm certainly not going to overdo it. I worked hard to get back here, to do for myself, and I won't be treated like an invalid, either. I know my limits. Now where is the rest of my family? They flew all this way and then scattered as soon as I made it down the stairs. They barely said hi."

But that wasn't entirely true. She hadn't missed how Brad, Neil, and Jed hovered on the steps, waiting to catch her if she fell. All eyes had been on her as she walked with her cane, one hand on Rodney's arm as he led her through the foyer and down the two steps into the sunken living room.

"Dad said he didn't want you getting overwhelmed, that you'd just gotten home and asked for everyone to go outside and give you some space," Neil said. He looked to Candy again. "I think Jed and Brad are in the pool with the kids."

The pool had been used less and less since the storm. Maybe she'd get back into swimming, too. That would certainly help along with her physical therapy.

She noticed how different Candy and Neil were with each other now. It seemed as if there was something solid where there hadn't been before. What was it about them that appeared stronger, closer? Before her stroke, she'd worried about whether Candy and Neil would make it. They had been so unsuited at one time. The deception, what Neil had done with that surrogate, lying to Candy when Michael was really his…Becky had wanted to say something to the two of them, take them aside, but her better sense had kicked in. This was their fight, and only they could work it out, just like she and Rodney had.

"Well, you tell your dad that I don't need anyone keeping my family away from me. Or maybe I need to go outside and tell him myself." She reached for her cane and started to get up, determined to put an end to this nonsense. The last thing she wanted was anyone, especially her husband, treating her as an invalid.

"No, Mom, stay there." Neil sounded almost frantic, and she could see that pushing him wasn't going to get him to stop worrying about her. "I'll go talk to Dad." He gave Candy a look, and she nodded, her expression guarded as if she understood his concern. He left with their baby.

"So what is that about?" Becky asked her daughter-in-law, who was still standing beside her. She gestured to the sofa. "Sit down, Candy. You're making me crane my neck to look all the way up at you."

"Sure," Candy replied. She curled her legs under her on the sofa, leaning on the arm, and smiled over at Becky.

"You and I haven't had much of a chance to talk."

Candy lowered her hand and smoothed her palm over the floral pattern on the cushions. Becky knew she loved the colors, the cherry red with green leaves and the cream background. It really added something to this room. "We were so worried about you."

"And I was worried about you and my son," Becky said, wondering when the best time would be to talk to Candy, woman to woman, about where she and Neil were as a couple.

Candy looked up, and for a moment there was surprise in her expression before she glanced over her shoulder to the doorway. "We're good. You don't need to worry about us."

Becky sighed. "I stayed out of it even though I wanted to sit you both down and talk to you…before the stroke. Afterward, it was so frustrating having to rely on Rodney. So much of what I wanted to say, I couldn't get the words out. But you two now seem happy, maybe content?"

Becky knew, by the way Candy was looking at her, that she was remembering the secret Rodney had shared, her indiscretion at a time when she believed nothing would ever work out.

"Yes, I suppose you and Rodney gave me a lot to think about," she replied. "I could see past my own hurt after that. I love Neil, and that will never change. I just never expected…I don't know, Becky. Hearing about your troubles when you were young, about how you and Rodney made that choice to make it work and find a way to stay together, it helped. When your dad threatened to take you and the kids away if Rodney couldn't make him understand all the ways he loved you…I can't imagine the heartache you were both suffering at that time. You're so strong, and listening to Rodney tell me your story shook me up and made me really think about Neil and our family. I actually sat down and made a list myself."

"Oh, really? That sounds good. It is, isn't it?"

"Well, it made me really think. Neil is such a wonderful man. He was my everything until I got that letter from the surrogate and found out that Michael was actually his. My trust was destroyed. How can you rebuild after that? I didn't think it was possible to ever trust him again, and that hurt more than anything."

"And you do now?" She hoped she was right. Candy wasn't acting like a woman on her way out the door. Becky hoped not, anyway.

She shrugged. "He saved me when the storm swept in, and he stayed by my side. He's just that kind of man. Where I'm scared at times, he's confident. He loves our children, and after coming around about Cat, falling in love with our sweet little girl, he'd move heaven and earth for her. He'll be there for me no matter what. It may not always have been this way, but he's given up so much of himself and what he's loved for me, without me asking him. One of the hardest things for Neil is caring enough about what I think and feel to share with me before decisions are made, but he's really trying. I'm glad Rodney shared your story with me."

"No one else knows in the family, Candy. Rodney shared that with you because we knew you had one foot out the door. It was all he could think of at the time to make you stop and consider."

"You never told Neil?" Candy asked.

She shook her head. "No one knows. It was something I swore I'd never speak of, and I knew Rodney would never want anyone knowing. The boys wouldn't understand, and I couldn't bear them thinking poorly of me."

Candy started to shake her head as if to argue the point.

"No, Candy, we all do things when we're young and stupid, and even though people can be well meaning and sympathetic, we all have a little something that we shouldn't share with others. People judge because that's easier than looking yourself in the mirror and seeing everything you've messed up in your own life. Oh, I know you want to argue with me that Neil would understand, and maybe he would. But maybe he wouldn't. I don't want to see that in his eyes, the question that would always be there: How could I have done something so horrible?"

Maybe Candy understood, as she nodded.

"You love him," Becky said.

"Yes, more than I thought it was possible to love a man." She was tracing a tiny leaf etched in the fabric of the arm of the sofa. "I worry, though."

Candy didn't have to look up for Becky to realize there were tears misting in her eyes. She could see the stubbornness in her daughter-in-law as she blew out her breath. Candy was clearly determined not to cry after all she'd been through, losing her home and any chance of carrying a child herself, then Neil's lie that had nearly destroyed everything between them.

"What are you worried about?" Becky said.

"This may sound silly to you, but everything is so good, almost perfect, between me and Neil. He listens to me now. He hears me. I feel for the first time that we're in a marriage together, like a real partnership, and I know he loves me. With Cat and Michael, he loves them so much. He's an amazing father." She stopped talking and was biting her lower lip.

"You're worried that it could be too good to be true and that something is going to come out of nowhere and rip the ground right out from beneath your feet."

Candy glanced up fast, and her eyes widened in surprise.

"Oh, Candy, I understand better than you think. It's

not foolish to have those thoughts, but take my advice. If you spend your time worrying that something is going to go wrong, then you can't enjoy the special moments you have now."

There were footsteps and voices in the hallway, and Becky could see Candy considering. Their time to talk would have to wait, though, as she was surrounded by her grandkids wrapped in towels and dripping from the pool.

"Mom, please sit down," Jed said. He wasn't used to the heat, even this late in the day, with the sun setting in the sky, and he shook his head. His mother had been on death's doorstep three months earlier and was pushing herself harder than he liked. It was a miracle she was walking, talking, and the thought of Becky Friessen no longer being around scared him more than he could admit to anyone, even himself.

"Jed, let me go give Ana a hand in the kitchen," she replied. She was trying to get up from her chair around the large patio table where the family had enjoyed dinner together. Fitting eight chairs around the outdoor table had been great, and the kids had eaten together on a blanket on the grass, with Brad's eldest, Katy, twelve going on thirteen, watching all the younger ones and running after his two little boys, Danny and Christopher. His wife, Diana, joked that they were hell raisers, and he had to agree they were, at least now, at ages four and two.

"No, Mom, Jed's right. Sit down," Brad said from where he sat beside her. "You've been on your feet, trying to direct Ana with dinner and seeing to the kids. Just sit here and talk with us."

Neil was at the end and picked up the wine bottle, filling up his glass and then Brad's as he walked around. He said something to his wife, who came out of the house, holding the baby. They shared a moment before he kissed her and she walked back inside.

"I noticed how you let your wives all tend to your kids," Becky said. "I can't remember the last time I got to sit around with you three and just talk." She lifted her water glass and took a sip, bumping the plate before setting it back on the table. Then she frowned. "I should help Ana clear the table." She started to lift her plate on top of Brad's.

Jed could see his mom wasn't comfortable having everyone around her do everything. She was the one who always showed up to help out. "Mom, just let Diana and Emily look after cleaning up. Dad's in the kitchen, too. Besides, you've always been the one to organize and look after things. Just relax for once and let someone else wait on you," Jed said. He could hear the kids running and yelling and laughing in the yard, and then Diana, his gorgeous red-haired wife with the most amazing deep blue eyes he'd ever seen, came out in a simple pink sundress.

"Danny, Christopher!" she called out to where the kids were all playing, but she stopped beside Jed when he reached out for her arm. He could feel how tense she was before he pulled her a bit so she could lean over and kiss him, her short hair brushing his face. "I'm going to get the boys bathed and ready for bed."

"Diana, why don't you leave them for now? Let them work off all that energy after traveling all day. They're excited to see their cousins," Jed said. He was happy to have the older kids, Katy and even Trevor, who had autism, playing with the boys. Little Becky, Brad and Emily's youngest, at seven, was also a big help, especially because she kept Cat, the little deaf girl Neil and Candy had adopted, glued to her side. The kids had such fun. They really needed to bring the family together more often.

Diana frowned, and Jed could see that she wasn't entirely comfortable letting the boys run wild as they were, both barefoot in their shorts with chocolate smeared on their clothes from the ice cream they'd had for dessert.

"Hey, Katy," Neil cupped his hands around his mouth and shouted out. Brad's stepdaughter had her light colored hair up in a high ponytail, and it swung around as she stopped from the game of tag the kids were playing.

"Yeah?" she called out. She was wearing jean shorts, and a black spaghetti-strap tank top. Anyone could see how self-conscious she was crossing her arms over her small breasts just beginning to grow in her skinny chest. Jed had noticed, and he could see Brad had a few more grays mixed in his thick dark hair.

"Look after Danny and Christopher for your aunt Diana," Neil said.

Jed just stared at his brother. Neil could be such a smart-tass, giving a dashing smile as he glanced up at Diana. Jed had given Neil a second and third look when he arrived with the light beard he appeared to be growing. It was so unlike him.

"Okay," Katy called out before joining back in the game.

"See, Diana?" Neil said. "Stop worrying. Go inside and have some fun with Emily and Candy. You've got a built-in babysitter here, and the kids are having a blast. Let your boys run themselves out so they crash from pure exhaustion. Have a glass of wine. Ask Ana to grab another bottle from the wine cellar." He lifted the bottle and filled up Jed's empty glass.

"Whoa, enough. I think I'd rather have a beer."

"That's because you have no taste, brother dear," Neil said. Jed realized he really did look happy.

"Jed, keep an eye on them," Diana said, patting his shoulder.

"Diana, they're fine. Neil's right: They're having fun. Just let them play. You go and hang out with Candy and Emily. I can see the kids," he said. He could see she was going to argue for a minute, as she had been worrying more about the boys as of late.

"Fine," she said, not entirely happy, and started back to the house.

"What's that about?" Neil frowned as he watched her. Even Becky was watching Diana as she strode away. Something wasn't quite right.

"Oh, Diana's been worrying lately," Jed said. "Her mother stopped by."

"Oh. That doesn't sound good, Jed," Becky said. "Didn't you tell me Diana's mom was in jail, that she'd done some awful things? When did she get out?"

Neil had that look about him that was all big brother. "What in God's name could that woman want after what she did to Diana? I hope you didn't let her stay."

For a minute, Jed forgot how close Neil was to his wife. But then, if anything ever happened to him, his brother had promised he'd look after Diana. He didn't miss the concern Brad leveled his way, too, as he slipped his arm over the back of their mother's chair.

"No, I sent her on her way, but it shook Diana up, having Faye show up at our house. Hell, I was stunned at how she'd found Diana. Worse, I could see where my wife gets her looks. Her mother's a looker, but there's something cold about that woman, too, something snaky that makes me uneasy."

"What did she want?" Brad asked, frowning.

"Said she wanted to get to know Diana. She even played up the grandmother thing. And for a minute I saw something in my wife that I didn't like. I wonder if she'd have let that woman come in if I hadn't walked up to the house. It was as if this woman had a power over her and could make her do anything."

"She's her mother, Jed. Don't be so hard on Diana." Becky tapped the table with her hand. "It's a good thing you were there, though. I can't imagine what she went through as a child. She must have been so disillusioned. But we can't choose our parents, and as children we love our parents unconditionally whether they deserve it or not."

His mom surprised him sometimes. He didn't get it, and he hated Faye Claremont for the childhood horror Diana had survived. She had lost a baby sister who had her own set of challenges, and Jed knew the reality of watching her drunken, drug-dealing whore of a mother had to have been worse than the few stories she had shared with him. Her memories were a scar on her soul that he didn't think she'd ever recover from.

"Do you want me to talk to Diana?" Neil looked over his shoulder again toward the door as if ready to jump up and go in to take his wife aside.

He wondered if he scowled. "No, she's my wife, Neil. Don't you have your own to deal with?"

Neil turned slowly. "That's not what I meant, Jed."

The way he said it, Jed could tell Neil had been reminded of how he'd lied to Candy about the surrogate. He'd weaved a whole lot of secrets to have his family and keep his wife, but then, Jed didn't know what he'd do in the same situation. Sometimes, Neil was a mystery.

"I'm just saying, Diana is my wife. I'll work it out with her. She just needs some time, and it's good, too, that we're here, far enough away that I don't have to worry her mom will show up again."

"I don't know, Jed," Brad said, still lounging comfortably beside their mom. "If that was Emily's situation, I'd make sure that woman never showed her face on our doorstep."

"Really, you mean like when your ex showed up on your doorstep for Trevor's birthday and you let her in?" Neil said. "You made Emily feel—"

"I know what I made her feel, Neil." Brad slapped the table, cutting his brother off. "You don't need to bring that up. It's not the same thing."

For a minute, Jed wondered whether Brad was going to reach around their mom and grab Neil's shirtfront. Becky slapped her hand against Brad's chest.

"Just cool down, Brad," she said. "Sometimes, the way you three talk, I wonder if you're about to break into a fistfight."

"Mom, we wouldn't do that." Neil flashed her one of his dazzling smiles.

"I cleaned up enough bloody noses from you three." His mom didn't back down. "Especially you, Jed. You got pounded on by your brothers more times than I could count when you were growing up."

"Yeah, we did, didn't we? You think maybe that's why he is the way he is?" Brad joked to Neil, and they both laughed at his expense.

"You guys are assholes," Jed said before finishing off the wine and moving his glass away so Neil couldn't pour him another.

Even his mom was laughing softly. "Okay, enough, you three. Brad, how is Emily doing? In all this commotion today, I haven't had a chance to talk with her. She's been herding your kids around and then on the phone nonstop. She seems distracted." Becky patted Brad's arm.

Jed hadn't realized Emily was distracted. He thought she was just being a mom, but then, Emily was always on the kids, being a mother and raising an autistic child. Trevor was from Brad's first marriage, but no one would ever suspect that Emily was anything other than his mother. Maybe his mom was reading more into the situation than she should.

Brad glanced to the door, and his expression changed. Jed had seen that look a time or two and could tell something was up. Then Brad wiped his hand roughly over his face, and Jed could hear the scrape of his whiskers. Brad, too, was looking a little rough around the edges, needing to shave.

"She's worried about next year for Trevor. He starts a new school, and we're running out of options for his grade level, as high school starts at grade nine. Our school district has had so many changes—new people, new administrators who don't want to work with his program, his consultant, or us, for that matter. They want to do things their own way as if they have it all figured out." Brad leaned back, scraping the chair legs, and frowned. "Emily is taking it hard. She's been fighting with the school, the counselors, the principal. They say no, she argues and won't go away. She's become a thorn in their side, as one of the teachers said to her."

"That doesn't sound good, either, Brad," Neil said. "She's done so much for Trevor. Where would he be without her?" He probably understood more about Trevor's situation, living closer to Brad now in Hoquiam, than Jed did. Jed loved his brothers, but he also knew that once he said goodbye, he would always go back to his world, his life with Diana and the boys.

Brad's face darkened, and he shook his head. Jed knew everything Emily had done, including opening Brad's eyes so he could see that Trevor had autism, helping him understand when he couldn't see what had been right in front of him.

"So what does this mean for school? Are they not going to take him?" Neil asked.

"Oh, they'll take him, but it's a question of what they'll do for him, what support he'll have. They won't allow his current support worker to stay with him in high school. There are so many closed-minded people we're dealing with right now. Emily handles it better than me. I'm not as nice, but at least when we walk in the school together and I'm with her, they treat my wife with more respect. They're not as nice if she goes in alone.

"It's becoming very political. It's all about the money they get from the state for a child with autism," he said. "It's extra funding for the school, but the administrators can do anything with the money. The principal doesn't have to account to the parents. He can decide what resources he wants to use. It's frustrating when you don't have a voice, and it make me so angry to realize that Trevor is literally a dollar sign to them. Unfortunately, we're finding the older Trevor gets, and the more kids are now being diagnosed, the less willing schools are to work with us or his consultant, who's the one responsible for how far he's come. We had it good, or Trevor did, for so long, with a school and principal who understood what we were doing, who were willing to work with us."

"But you paid for the support, the therapy, the courses, everything, and the school benefited. I don't understand,

Brad. This is a no brainer for them to want to work with you and your consultant." Neil sounded irritated.

Jed didn't know what to make of it as he listened. He couldn't add anything, because if it were him, he'd go in demanding, not knowing what else to do. But it made sense now, Emily's distraction. He couldn't imagine Diana dealing with that, and he didn't know how he'd handle any of it if he were in Brad's shoes. Probably not well.

"We'd gladly continue to pay for services, support, anything we need to. We may have to consider home schooling, but that goes against everything Trevor needs socially."

"Well, what about a private school, Brad? That may be a better option," Neil said, looking around the table at all of them as if he already had some ideas.

"At the high school level, there isn't much around. I wish there was. There's more in the city, but I'm not packing my family up and moving there," Brad said. "We'll figure something out."

"Of course you will," Becky said. "You have a good woman in there who will make sure you're headed in the right direction. Sounds to me as if maybe it would be good for me to spend some time with my daughter-in-laws."

Jed wasn't sure what to make of that—but maybe that would be exactly what Diana needed: another woman, his mother, to talk to.

CHAPTER

Four

"Em, you're worrying yourself to death," Brad said. "Come to bed. There's nothing more you can do tonight. This is mom and dad's anniversary, so just try to put it out of your mind for now. You can't solve it from here."

Brad was in bed in the guest room where they always stayed when they came to Cancun to visit his parents. It had a small balcony with French doors that overlooked the swimming pool. Everything was yellow and white, with an easy chair in the corner. It was comfortable, or should have been, except for the fact that his wife was pacing the tile floor barefoot in her short blue nightgown. He loved how it draped to her thighs, the thin spaghetti straps and flattering cut teasing him with her cleavage. She ran her fingers through her shoulder-length brown hair. She was slender and curvy, and his body stirred just thinking of settling inside her.

"Brad, I can't. Do you know what that new principal said to me? He lost his temper on the phone when I called before leaving this morning, and he said he was tired of every parent coming in and telling him how to run his school. He was nasty."

Brad had a few choice words he planned on saying to that principal, considering he was close to retirement but just wouldn't budge. Maybe he needed to be the one to give the arrogant jerk the shove he needed. Whatever he decided, there was one thing this principal was going to learn really fast: Upsetting Brad's wife was a bad move.

He pulled the covers down on Emily's side and patted the mattress. "Come here, get in bed. Let it go for now. We can't do anything yet, and maybe there's some other options we can start looking at."

"What options?" She stiffened as she stopped pacing, her hands on her hips.

Did she have any idea what it did to him when she stood before him looking this way? Obviously not, by the way she appeared so frazzled.

"Em, I mean it. Get in bed." He wondered for a minute whether he'd have to get out of bed and get her— which he'd do if she didn't get her butt in bed in the next few seconds. He was tired, and he knew she hadn't been sleeping well, either, because every time she stirred in the night and tossed and turned, he woke up. Even her sighs as she struggled to sleep would wake him.

"Brad, you're not taking this seriously." She started toward him, obviously not having heard him. She was focused on talking, on venting her outrage about how twisted up this school crap was becoming. He'd had enough with the wasted energy and was thinking more and more about finding other options.

"I'm taking this very seriously, Em, but I'm not about to worry it to death and ruin our time with the family. I don't want to talk about this anymore."

He wondered for a moment whether she was going to

argue with him, as she stiffened as if getting ready to fight. Any fight she had, he wanted to feel it under him, with the passion that burned between them. When she didn't move but appeared to be thinking about how mad she was, he threw back the covers and climbed out of bed naked.

Of course she could see he wanted her, and what did she do in response but cross her arms and actually look at him as if she was going to deny him? The day she said no to Brad, and the day she wasn't interested in making love with him and connecting the way they did, would be the day he truly realized they were in trouble.

He scooped her up, and she shrieked, looping her arms around his neck. He dumped her on the bed, her legs dangling over the side, and stood over her, looking down at her. She was breathing heavy, her chest rising and her eyes locked on to his. He took her legs and pressed them open, watching her as he ran his hand down her thighs to her knees. Her eyes took on that heated look, and he knew he was breaking through her resolve. She couldn't fight him, not like this.

He ran his hand up the soft skin of her inner thigh again to her nakedness. She was so warm for him, and her breath hissed when he touched her. He didn't say a word as he watched his wife watching him. How much would it take to get her to let go? He pressed the palm of his hand to her and could feel how wet she was. Then he slipped his hand under her nightgown, sliding up over her slender stomach and higher still.

He grabbed the hem of her nightgown and lifted it up to pull it over her head as she sat up for him, and he tossed it to the side. He could see how her breasts appeared to be waiting for his taste, his touch, as if begging him to take a nipple in his mouth. She was so on edge, he realized, that if he slid his finger inside her, she'd probably come off the bed. So he ran his hand down her stomach and then over her hip, purposely not touching her where she was begging him to. She moved her hips as he skimmed down the outside of her leg.

"Brad…" Her voice squeaked, and she raised her hips up, circling them and spreading her legs wider. He stepped away, and for a minute he thought she was going to reach for him and try to pull him back.

He couldn't help the sly smile that pulled at his lips. She was so fired up and distracted, and before she could move any further, he stepped into her, taking her knees and pushing them out as he filled her hard and fast.

"Oh, Brad, oh my God," she cried out as he moved again, hard and fast, rustling her on the bed as he held her legs wide. His hands wrapped around her knees as he continued to move again inside her. He didn't take his eyes off the heat, the want and desire burning for him as he moved his hips, slapping against her softness.

"Put your arms above your head, Em," he growled and watched as she reached up, squirming beneath him.

She turned her head to the side and closed her eyes, and he could tell she was fast losing herself in the feel of him, so he pulled out. "Brad, no, please…" she begged as she went to reach for him.

"No, look at me, arms up. You watch me, and you look at me. Don't turn away."

She was at a point where he knew she'd do anything he asked of her. Right now, he was going to take her over the edge so she could forget everything but this moment and them. He grabbed her hips this time and wasn't gentle when he moved inside her, faster, harder, riding her to the point of being rough. But he knew she loved it, that she could take it. She was a woman who could keep up with him, his woman, whom he could never get enough of.

He could feel her starting to come apart under him, and knowing her so well and how she responded to him, he knew the moment right before she cried out. He probably understood her body and how she responded to his touch better than she did. He moved harder, taking her with him over the edge, connecting their souls closer, he swore, than it was possible for two people to ever connect. Then he collapsed on top of her.

"Are the kids asleep?" Candy asked. She was sitting at the small writing desk in their massive bedroom, which could have been a suite in itself, with a massive four-poster and a new sectional in front of a fireplace that Neil couldn't remember ever having been used. He loved the colors, the red and gold, the dark wood, and the local native art covering the walls.

"Bathed, fed, watered, and tucked in for the night," he replied. "Cat was out by the time her head hit the pillow, snuggled in beside little Becky, and she was out, too, by the time I finished that last story. Michael dropped off to sleep before he finished his bottle."

Neil loved his children and enjoyed these moments when he could be a part of their lives, doing the small things he realized his brothers never did. He kicked off his sandals, feeling gritty from the humid heat that had blasted in. It was as if Cancun had only two seasons: summer and summer. Then again, there was also the stormy season.

Candy was watching him as she slid around in that straight-backed chair, putting the pen she was holding down on top of the small diary she'd started writing in. Instead of closing it this time, she left it open, her hand resting on the side of the hardcover book. Maybe she noticed the way he took in the book and her neat penmanship as he walked toward her.

"Good," she replied. She was looking at him, and he could see the vulnerability and shyness in her, which would surface at the oddest times. He stopped right beside her, touching her bare shoulder. She was stunning even in shorts and a tank top. She was slim and curvy, and he loved her long, straight hair even though she insisted on pulling it back and knotting it on top of her head. He reached behind and unclipped it, and the silky strands slipped past her shoulders and down her back. Her hair was long enough to reach her waist, and he loved running his hands through it.

He slid both hands over her cheeks, holding her face as he leaned down and kissed her, allowing his lips to linger for a few seconds. He didn't push the kiss, pulling back just enough to rub his nose with hers and feel her warm breath mix with his.

Candy slid her hand over his wrist as he watched her. Her dark eyes could, at times, smolder with a fire that turned from passion to anger so fast it made his head spin. He had seen enough anger from her when she thought she hated him, back before the storm. The passion was something he brought to life every time he had her under him or when she rode him, slow and easy, in the morning before either was really awake. His woman was complicated, anything but simple, even though he knew she believed she was ordinary. No, his Candy was the best. She was the world to him. She was a single-malt whiskey that was smooth and burning, one he could appreciate. He wondered whether she'd ever believe how good she was. At one time, he knew she believed she wasn't good enough for him, but the truth was that he wasn't good enough for her. She was the prize.

"You all right?" She gave him an odd look and ran her hand up his arm. He loved it when she touched him.

"Of course. Was just thinking how lucky I am."

"Oh?" She smiled up at him and left her book open as she stood, putting her hand on the flat of his chest and stepping closer so he could wrap his arms around her. She fit so perfectly, and he could have looked down at her book and read it, he was so close. But he couldn't do that to her. The diary was hers, her thoughts, something personal and private. He knew he couldn't cross that line—even though he wanted to know everything she was thinking at every moment.

"You love writing in that book," he said. "What is it you put down in there?"

Candy couldn't hide from him, and he could sense the moment she felt uneasy. It was so subtle, the change in her body, from leaning into him, her energy reaching out and touching him, to pulling away. He rubbed her back and lower, over her sweet ass, holding her to him, not hard but in a way that let her know she could step away if she wanted. He wanted her with him, always, to stay close to him, but it had to be her choice. That nearly killed him at times, but the saying was "If you love someone, set her free, for if she truly loves you, she will always return." For Neil right now, because of what he'd done, he'd learned that with Candy, it was so true. He couldn't push, not ever again.

She was pulling her lower lip in between her teeth, so he reached up and ran his thumb over it until she let it go. "You'll think it's silly," she said.

"No, I don't think it's silly. It's important to you, it

means something to you, so it's important to me. Nothing you ever do is silly."

She appeared surprised by what he said. He wondered whether him being so possessive of her, attempting to rearrange things for her, taking care of everything, had made her think he wouldn't share her interests. She opened her mouth to say something, and he could feel her relax against him as she slid her hand up his chest. He could feel the slight tremble in her hand.

"You don't have to share it," he said.

Her eyes darted up so fast. He could see the surprise, maybe because he'd always pushed, expecting her to share everything, body, mind, and soul. He still wanted that, but something had changed when he'd hurt her with his betrayal—his secrets.

No more, ever.

"They're just my thoughts, feelings," she said, and she didn't need to say any more. He could tell she expected him to push.

"These are things you don't want to share with me?" He had to know, to have some idea of where she was in her head with him, just to understand where they still needed to go to heal.

"You'd think they're silly, I'm sure. I'd feel foolish voicing them, but I want to be able to put it down. It helps me," she whispered.

He nodded although he couldn't help feeling a little hurt that she didn't want to share everything with him. He also knew he couldn't push, not anymore.

"Thank you," she said.

"For what?"

"For not pushing, for not insisting on reading it. You've never looked at it, have you?"

Before, he would have. That was the old Neil, who was

so obsessed with having Candy and molding her into who he believed she should be. What a fool he'd been. "No, I wouldn't do that, although I am curious," he teased.

She slid her hand around his waist and slapped his butt playfully, hugging him closer. She had the most beautiful smile as she leaned in and tilted her head up, again biting her lower lip. "Maybe one day I'll show you."

What could he say to that? She watched him with a lightness in her eyes that melted away the uncertainty that had been between them moments ago. He wanted her to trust him again. Oh, he knew she did in some things, but he wanted that ultimate trust where she would believe that her precious, vulnerable heart would be safe with him regardless of what life threw their way. If and when she trusted him completely again, he swore to God that he would never let her down again.

"I would love that," he said.

Six

" I would feel better if the boys were in here with us," Diana said. She was brushing out her boyish short red hair. Jed had always loved her hair, her long, silky, vibrant red locks. She had always worn it down, that is, until her mother showed up—a woman with the same vibrant hair and big blue eyes as her daughter. Seeing her mother had rocked her world in ways Jed hadn't realized, and the very next day, Diana had driven into town and cut all her hair off. He'd been shocked that she hadn't run it by him, but then again, his response would have been "Hell, no!"

There'd been something about those silky long locks. He had loved dragging his hands through them, winding up those long tresses in his fingers and holding her to him. The last time she'd gotten down on her knees and tasted him, he'd gripped her long hair in his fist and held her there. He mourned the loss.

"The boys are fine where they are," he replied. They were bunking with their cousins, Trevor and Katy. Christopher had actually fallen asleep cuddled up to Katy in the double bed at the bottom of the set of bunk beds. The top bunk Trevor had taken, and he'd been quietly talking to himself, or "stimming," as Katy had mentioned. She'd told him once to stop, and Jed had been surprised at how compliant he was and how good Katy was with him. He'd noticed a strong unbreakable bond between Katy and Trevor. Danny, meanwhile, was on a blowup mattress in the corner, covered with the yellow bumblebee blanket he loved. It was the one he'd spotted in the closet when the beds were being made. He'd fallen in love with the thin quilt, claimed it, and was now sound asleep underneath it.

Diana put the brush down on the white dresser. The guest room they stayed in was the smallest one in this massive estate, but it was still about half the size of their small ranch house in Snohomish County. It was very comfortable, opening onto a private balcony. Diana was staring down at the brush, distracted, and Jed could feel how tightly she was wound from where he stood. He stepped closer until he was right behind her. If he pulled her back, he could have rested his chin on her head. She fit so perfectly against him, as if she'd been made just for him. He ran his hand down her bare arm, over the light freckles that were popping up from their day outside.

"You look as if you've had too much sun. You're pink here," he said, tracing his callused fingers over her bare shoulder and the thin straps of her sundress. He noticed then that she was watching him in the mirror. Oh, yes, there was a heaviness there in her gaze as if she were carrying the weight of the world.

"I'll wear sunscreen tomorrow," she snapped, irritated, and made no move to lean against him. She was holding herself stiff, still gripping the brush so hard her hand was white.

"What's going on, Diana?"

She sighed and lowered her gaze, first lifting the brush and then letting it topple from her hand. It clattered on the white dresser, and she stepped away from Jed even when he tried to hold on to her. He could feel her tension.

"Diana," he said a little sternly, not knowing how else to reach her.

"You won't understand." She kept her back to him. He'd never seen her like this, and it was frustrating the hell out of him, not knowing how to pull her out of it. He'd love to just grab her shoulders and shake her, but then she'd shut down.

"Try me. I'm your husband, remember?" Maybe he said it a little rougher than he'd meant to.

"I know you are." She turned around. Her short skirt stopped just above her knees. She still had a great body after giving him two babies. She was still slim, but he'd swear her ample breasts were bigger now than before she'd had his children. He realized she wasn't wearing a bra. Maybe he frowned, or his expression was off, because her hands went up, and she crossed her arms over her breasts.

She looked away.

"Diana, don't shut me out—and since when do you walk around without a bra, especially around my family?" He didn't like the fact that her nipples were poking through the thin pink cotton. If he could see the outline…good grief, had his brothers, too?

"I'm sorry. I forgot to pack the strapless bra. I thought it would be okay." She looked genuinely hurt.

"Look, Diana, ever since your mom showed up, you've been worried about something, and I don't know what it is. I don't know what to do. It's as if she flipped some switch, and you're worrying and stressing about something."

She turned away, and he could see how tightly she'd fisted her hands across her bust. She was shaking, not hard, but just enough that when she finally turned around, he'd swear she was trying to hide herself. He could see her tears.

"I don't want to be my mother, Jed. I don't want to be anything like her." Her mouth trembled.

"Diana, you're not your mother. Why would you even think for a moment that you are?"

A stray tear slipped from the corner of her eye. She lifted her hand from her breast and roughly wiped it away before it could fall. He could tell she was fighting back a sob.

What was going on with her?

"Even you said a minute ago about the way I was dressed, with no bra…I must look like trash. She's a whore, and I look just like her!" she cried out.

"Diana," he snapped and strode toward her, putting his hands on her shoulders and holding her even when she shook her head and tried to back away. "Don't put words in my mouth. You are not trash. You are my wife. I just meant I'm not happy my brothers or anyone, for that matter, is getting a look at these." He put his hands over her amazing breasts. As far as he was concerned, they were his to play with, to touch, to taste, and he would be the only man to ever see them—ever. "You are stunning," he said, "and you are not your mother."

She dropped her head against his chest, and he could feel her shaking as if she was fast losing her battle against the tears. She rubbed her face against his chest and sniffed loudly. Jed put his hand around the back of her head, holding her against him, and pressed a kiss into the top of her head.

"Diana, you need to believe what I'm saying. Listen to me. You're so kind and loving. You are the best mother to Danny and Christopher. I could see how rattled you were when Faye showed up. I don't want her messing with you again, so whatever crap is going through your head where you think you're anything like her, well, you just shake it off."

She nodded roughly against him and sniffed, resting her chin against his chest while looking up at him. Her face was red and blotchy from the tears she was holding back.

"Look at you," he said, wiping away the dampness on her face and taking in the tiny lines around her eyes, which seemed a little more deeply etched. It was worry, was all. And maybe this time away, this distance from home, would give her back the peace she deserved.

CHAPTER

Seven

"Your mom is still resting. I didn't want to wake her," Rodney said.

Neil took in his dad, neatly dressed in khakis and a white golf shirt that contrasted against his tan. Rodney Friessen was a handsome man. His gray hair also had that freshly cut look, but then, Neil was pretty sure his dad had stopped to get his hair cut before picking up his mom from the rehab center the day before.

"So how did you sleep?" Neil was barefoot and reached for one of the dark green mugs set on a platter in front of the coffeepot.

"Good, I guess." His dad shrugged as he poured some cream into his coffee, stirring it with a spoon and tapping it on the edge before putting it in the sink.

Neil looked over at his dad. They'd always been the same height, but he wondered whether his dad had shrunk a bit. "You worried about Mom?" Neil asked, because ever since the stroke, he'd watched his father come down early in the morning every day, and the first thing he would do was grab his keys and go to the rehab center where his mom was to start his day with his wife.

"She pushed herself yesterday. You know your mom, she won't slow down. I was worried about her last night, though I shouldn't have been, as she slept so soundly."

The way his dad said it, Neil could tell something was bothering him. How much could he pry from his dad? His father was not a talker or sharer of his feelings. Rodney Friessen was the head of their family, never the vulnerable one, but Neil had seen something in his dad that scared him the first time he walked in that hospital room and watched him sitting beside his mother's bedside after her stroke. His dad had appeared old for the first time as he watched over her. It was then that Neil knew how much it would destroy his father if Becky Friessen didn't pull through. He loved her deeply.

"Don't worry about it, son." Rodney reached out and patted Neil's shoulder. "It's just good to have your mom home. I didn't think this day would come. It's all she's talked about, what she's looked forward to all this time." His father glanced up when they heard footsteps in the quiet house. Everyone must have been tired, as it was after seven. Even Neil had left Candy fast asleep in bed. It wasn't the first time he'd slipped out of bed and left her to sleep, even though he much preferred waking her with his body, making love to her while he was still half asleep. He knew she loved it, too, by the soft sounds she made. After last night, they'd spent their time in bed wrapped in each other's arms. And he'd just held her.

"Good morning," Jed said as he wandered in, his short brown hair sticking up. He was wearing yesterday's T-shirt with a pair of blue jeans and was carrying Christopher, his two-year-old little boy, who had Diana's eyes and Jed's smile.

"Well, you look as if someone dragged you out of bed," Neil said. He couldn't resist, considering Jed always did look a little rough around the edges.

"Christopher, here, appeared right beside the bed," Jed explained. "I brought him down so he wouldn't wake Diana. How about some cereal, bud?"

"Yeah. I want corn flakes," Christopher said.

"Corn flakes…I don't know what Ana's got, but check in the pantry," Rodney said. "Or ask Neil, here. He probably knows better than me. If you two will excuse me, I'm going to take my coffee upstairs and see if your mother is awake."

Neil watched as his dad left with his mug and picked up the newspaper that was sitting on the edge of the counter. He glanced over at his brother, who was also watching his dad walk out of the kitchen.

"Everything okay?" Jed asked as Christopher leaned over, trying to get down.

"With Dad? I think so. You were asking about Dad, right?" Neil opened the door to the pantry and pulled out a box of cereal. His dad was right about one thing: He knew how well the house was stocked—not because of Ana but because he made sure they had everything they needed. Those were the organizational skills he'd always excelled at. He sat the box on the counter. "Bowls are in that cupboard. I'll grab the milk."

He followed Jed to the table and put the carton of milk down. Jed poured his son a bowl of cereal and then poured himself a coffee, dumping in some milk from the carton on the table. He used his finger to stir it, and Neil couldn't help shaking his head as he looked down at the pile of clean spoons on the tray with the mugs.

"I was actually asking about you and Candy, but it's good to know Dad's doing well." Jed gestured with his mug to Neil before taking a swallow. "Where are you and Candy at?"

Neil put his mug down on the counter and leaned down on his arms. "We're, uh…" He wanted to say "good"—no, "great"—but he also couldn't help worrying that although they'd come so far, there was still a long way to go. "One day at a time," he said.

Jed was watching him as if trying to read between the lines of what he was saying, but Neil didn't want to talk about his screw-ups anymore. At some point in time, everyone would have to let it go and move on. That was what they all needed to do, what he needed to do, and it was what both he and Candy were trying to do. Every time his family asked, though, he wondered whether they were thinking he had done something stupid to fuck everything up again.

"Good, that sounds workable." Jed swallowed the last of his coffee and then reached for the pot to refill his cup. His brother always could down the coffee, food, anything, and be out the door before everyone else sat down.

"What about you and Diana?" He said it low enough that Christopher couldn't hear. "She seemed upset still, distracted, overly worried, or was that my imagination?"

Jed glanced over at his son and put the empty coffee pot back on the burner. "I should make some more."

Neil reached for the clay jar Ana stored the coffee in and slid it toward Jed, then gestured to the garbage under the sink, where he could dump the grounds. He watched as his brother made another pot of coffee and seemed to be considering what to say about his wife. Jed could be so closed mouthed, unwilling to share anything at times, but Neil also knew that the sun, the moon, and everything, as far as Jed was concerned, shone on Diana. He loved her, he worried about her.

"Diana's mom showing up was a mind fuck for her. I can't even get into her head to try to reason with her. You know her mom was Uncle Todd's plaything, and you also know how Diana suffered because of Andy and Todd as a kid. Even when she came back, they saw her as her mother. And then her mom showing up before we came here…I saw in Diana's eyes this hurt I've never seen before, and that was after I chased her mother away. I think Diana was terrified. She's really shaken up. I just can't figure out how she's gotten it into her head that she's somehow like her mother."

Neil didn't know what to say. He'd have to sit Diana down and talk to her, help her see what a giving, beautiful, loving woman she was. She wasn't just his sister-in-law, she was his friend. Neil didn't know Faye, but he knew enough of what Diana had endured as a child, the bits and pieces told from Jed and his cousin, Andy. It was sick and twisted, and she'd been just a little kid caught in the middle of a war between her mother and Todd.

"So what are you going to do?" Neil asked. He knew what he'd do: He'd hunt that woman down and find a way to make sure she left town and never came back. He didn't care what people would think. That was what you did to protect the ones you loved.

Jed glanced over his shoulder to his little boy, who was tipping the cereal bowl back and drinking the milk down, most of it dripping on his striped pajama top. "I don't rightly know yet, but I'll be damned if Faye Claremont is ever going to get the chance to mess with my wife again."

The look in his brother's amber eyes was enough for Neil to know he would do whatever it took to protect Diana and his boys. "If you need any help, you know where to come," he said.

Jed just watched him for a moment. His expression was

guarded. Sometimes, Neil didn't know what the hell to make of Jed or what he was thinking. Then he said, "You, too, Neil."

CHAPTER

Eight

Becky wasn't sure what to make of Rodney hovering over her. When she opened her eyes, it took her a moment to remember where she was. The room was bright, and a newspaper rustled, and she looked over to see Rodney sitting in an easy chair—but this wasn't the sterile environment of the rehab center. It was their bedroom, and she was home.

"Please tell me you haven't been sitting here waiting for me to wake up?" Her voice sounded deep and husky, the words a little slurred.

Damn, the man looked good as he lowered the paper. She, on the other hand, had to look a sight. After all these years, she was worrying again.

"Not that long," he replied. "I thought I should be here in case you needed something. Your nurse will be here at nine."

She'd forgotten Nola was coming back. The nurse was nice enough, dark haired, middle aged, with a young family. But she was a stranger. "I don't need her, Rodney. Why don't you call her and tell her not to come?" Becky slid back the covers to find that her nightgown had ridden up. She took her time sitting up and putting her feet on the floor. Her cane was resting beside the bed, and she caught a look of horror in Rodney's expression.

"Of course you need her. Don't be silly."

Becky needed to use the bathroom, and she had no desire to drag this out. "Rodney, Nola is just going to get in my way, I'm going to have a shower, and then I'd like to go down for breakfast to see my kids and start planning this anniversary dinner." She leaned on her cane to stand up about the same time Rodney was out of the chair, reaching for her.

"You don't need to do this all yourself, Becky. You only just got home. I've asked Nola to come every day to help you get started."

"Well, un-ask her."

"You can't shower yourself!" Rodney could shout when he wanted to, but it was fear she picked up in his voice, not anger.

"Yes, I can. Stop worrying. I'm fine."

"I'm not going to stop worrying. You have no idea what that did to me when I found you on the floor when you had your stroke. You scared the hell out of me. You almost didn't make it, and I'm not ready for you to go. We've had only forty-five years, and I want more." He really was upset.

She sat back on the bed and looked at her husband, who had appeared so composed a moment before. The wildness in his soft blue eyes was something she'd hadn't seen in years. It was a fear of something that could possibly be ending, something that neither wanted to be over.

"I'm sorry, Rodney. We're going to have many more years together. I'm not giving up. I'm here, I'm getting stronger every day, and there's a lot I can do myself."

"I don't want you to push yourself when you don't have to."

He really didn't understand, and she wasn't sure how to get through to him. "Rodney, my dear husband, I do not want to be waited on or to be pampered or to have some strange woman gawking at my naked ass while I shower. I will push myself because I can, and I know I can do something when I'm determined, but I'm not going to overdo it. If I need help, I'll ask for it." *Maybe,* she thought. She'd be dammed if she'd have anyone bathing her again or cleaning her intimates after she went to the bathroom. It was humiliating. That was why she'd pushed herself so hard, so she could once again be a wife to her husband. It worried her to think for one moment that she could be a burden. She wanted her husband, on this anniversary, to look at her as he always had, as the woman he married— the woman he still loved.

"Maybe you don't get it," Rodney said. "You took years off me, finding you barely alive. It brought back that day when I walked in our front door and saw the blood covering both your arms. You were standing there, in front of Brad and Neil, and you had that look as if you'd given up on everything. I thought you'd given up again!" he shouted, and there were tears in his eyes. He was such a strong, proud man, and she'd shaken him to the core.

"Rodney, I'm not that scared, stupid young girl you married anymore. I'm sorry, but that was forty years ago. You and I both did things we shouldn't have, and I wish I could go back and undo what I did, but I can't—and I'd never just leave like that. I love you. I love our children, my grandkids. Have a little more faith in me." She hoped she was getting through to him.

"I know you wouldn't. I'm just telling you I need the peace of mind of knowing you're all right. All I'm asking for is for you to let the nurse I hired help you in the mornings, at least."

Could she deny him? She was considering letting him win. She didn't want him to worry, but she couldn't stand for him to see her as weak or, worse, as an invalid who had to be cared for. She needed him to see her as his wife, capable, strong, and able to do all she once had. She had pushed herself to walk, to move, fighting against her body's unwillingness to cooperate. After waking up in the hospital after trying to slit her wrists, she told herself she'd never go back to rock bottom, and that day, she, Becky Ann Neilson, as she still considered herself, the spoiled, insecure child of Charles and Betty Neilson who'd grown up in the Napa Valley and married one of the Friessen men, had died. And Becky Ann Friessen, wife to Rodney Friessen, had begun to live.

"No." She held up her hand when she saw how tightly wound her husband was. She could see his frustration at being unable to reason with her, but then, he should know, after all these years, that Becky was tough as nails. She was as vulnerable as the next, but once she made up her mind, he'd have a better chance of trying to convince the wind to change direction. He often teased her about this when he calmed down after seeing reason whenever she dug her heels in. "But—so you won't worry, as I can see how this is distressing you—I'll let you send in Candy, Diana, or Emily."

Of course he wasn't happy. His expression was plain as day as he shook his head and started toward the door. Becky just smiled as she leaned on her cane and started walking to the bathroom.

CHAPTER

Nine

"I don't know why your mother is pulling this now," Rodney said. "Sometimes I think she believes she has to be invincible, but she's not."

Brad didn't know what to say as he listened to his dad rant. Rodney was someone who didn't carry on and on, but then, Becky had been the one to center the family, the force that kept them together. She was the one who always tried to smooth things over, who arranged their time together, and who also knew when to step in and when to stay out of something that was not her business. It could be that his mom's stroke had left his dad scrambling to find his feet. They had such a strong marriage, they were friends, and he wondered at times if they each knew what the other was thinking.

"Señor, breakfast is ready. It's set out in the dining room so everyone can serve themselves," Ana, the house-keeper, said. She had set out a buffet in the silver warmers, and Brad could smell the coffee, eggs, sausage, and another spicy aroma. His stomach growled as he breathed it in. He was starving, especially after the night he'd spent loving his wife.

"Dad, Mom has always done it all. It was hard for all of us to see her taken out. I don't understand, though, why she doesn't want her nurse. Nola's there to help." Maybe he would talk to Neil about the nurse, since he and Candy had stayed on at the estate with their parents after the stroke. Brad had been stopping in and keeping an eye on Neil and Candy's new home, their acreage outside Hoquiam, where Brad and Emily lived. That was what family did.

He heard voices and footsteps and chatter as the women came into the kitchen, His mom was dressed in tan capris, sandals on her feet, and a green T-shirt. She even appeared to be wearing a touch of makeup. She was using her cane but walking well with Candy beside her. Emily and Diana were following, chatting with each other. He noticed then that his mom looked happy and not as pale as the day before.

"Well, she looks good, Dad, you've got to admit," he said, because she did. His mom didn't appear to need any help walking as she listened to something Candy was saying. The women all looked as if this were any other day and being summoned to their mom's room to help in some way was nothing out of the ordinary.

"Rodney, dear, would you pour me a coffee?" his mom asked as she kept walking with Candy, who looked more settled than Brad had seen her in a long time. She was in a black tank top and white skirt, sandals on her feet. Diana was in shorts and a T-shirt, pale blue, and his wife had decided to throw on a sundress, wine colored, that stopped just above her knees. She also appeared far more relaxed now.

Brad reached out for Emily and pulled her from Diana,

who gave him an odd look but then kept on walking. He could see the kids, Jed, and Neil come in from the patio. There was clatter and laughing and the sounds of everyone digging in to the food.

Rodney said nothing else as he, too, left Emily and Brad alone in the kitchen.

"So what happened with Mom? When Dad came down, he seemed quite upset that she wouldn't allow him to have her nurse here."

Emily glanced into the dining room, and Brad followed the direction she was looking, which was toward his mom, who was now smiling and sitting in her spot at the large dining table. Neil leaned down and kissed her cheek, the baby in his arms.

Emily waved her hand. "Your mom was just keeping your dad happy. We didn't do a thing, just sat around. I have to admit, though, I'm a little surprised your mom is getting around as well as she is. She's slow, but she insisted she didn't need help. I asked. We just talked."

Emily looked up at him, her blue eyes seeming free of the worry she'd been carrying since arriving in Cancun. "I have to admit, it was kind of nice, just the four of us with your mom, spending time together." She let out a sigh and then smiled again. "I don't think you have to worry too much. Even the stairs she managed herself. We tried to help, but she just lifted her cane, held on to the rail, and went down one foot at a time. She's determined. I admire her."

He didn't know what to say to that. Maybe Emily understood his concern, as she reached for his hand and tugged. "Come on, stop overthinking this. Let's just enjoy this time here. Isn't that what you said to me last night?"

"Yeah, but it took a lot more than talk for me to get you to let it go, if you remember."

Of course she remembered. He could feel her response as her body moved closer to him on instinct. She couldn't fight the connection between them, his own body stirring from her touch and the last time he'd had her that morning, waking her as he entered her from behind, holding her to him.

"Hmm," she murmured as she went into his arms. He slid his hand behind her head and into her silky hair, holding her as he pressed a kiss to the top of her head. He rocked with her in his arms for a moment, and she pressed a kiss to his chest.

"Hey, you two, would you knock it off and get in here for breakfast?" Neil called out, a baby on his hip, a plate in his hand.

"Coming," Brad said. He slipped his arm around Emily and turned her, and they started into the dining room together. He didn't miss how his dad appeared to be waiting on his mom, making a plate filled with eggs, sausage, and fresh fruit. His mom, though, seemed to not give it much notice as she took a sip of her coffee and put the mug down. He did notice the slight tremble in her hand and wondered if his dad had, too. Jed and Diana followed the kids outside to where a table had been set up for them.

"After breakfast, I think it would be a good idea if I take my daughter-in-laws to the new spa at your resort, Neil. My treat," Becky said. "The four of us can plan this anniversary party. Neil, you can call and make arrangements, and you boys can stay here with your dad and spend time with my grandkids."

It was the first time Brad had seen Neil speechless, as he froze with a forkful of eggs midway to his mouth. Brad held Emily a little closer, his hand tightening on her waist, and Candy was staring at Neil.

"Ah, Mom, that may not be possible. You see…" Neil cleared his throat and exchanged another look with Candy. For a minute, Brad felt his chest tighten, worrying that his brother had done something else to mess up and kept yet another secret from his wife.

Candy was across the table, leaning over Cat, adjusting her cochlear implant behind her ear. She moved the little girl's glass of juice back from the table edge so she didn't spill it. "Becky," she began, "Neil is selling the resort, and there's a new buyer there now who's considering the purchase as he goes through the day-to-day operations." Candy lifted her gaze across the table, first to Neil and then Becky. "He may feel awkward arranging something considering the time of year, too, as the occupancy rate is over eighty percent."

Brad was stunned as he listened to Candy explain Neil's business. Not only did she seem to understand more than he did, but this was the first he was hearing about a new buyer since Neil talked about selling at Christmas.

"Oh?" Becky said and turned to Neil, having to shuffle a little more as she slid around in her chair. "Selling, since when?"

His mom was sharp, looking around at all of them. She had to be wondering whether he knew, too. Brad glanced at Jed as he walked in, his expression confused as he picked up on the quietness that had come over the dining room.

"Is someone going to explain to me what's going on?" Becky asked, this time looking to their dad.

"We should maybe speak of this later" was all Rodney said. Candy was resting her arm over Cat's chair, and the little girl was looking up at her mom while stuffing a pancake in her mouth.

"Mom, it's complicated, but…" Neil gestured with one hand to Candy, as Michael was in his arms, making baby cooing sounds as he patted Neil's face. He quickly, and noisily kissed Michael's chubby cheek. "It's what Candy and I want. We're going back soon to our place outside Hoquiam."

"That resort was all you talked about for years," Becky said. "It was one of the things that kept you and Candy apart for so long, and, Candy, that was your father's land, what he left you. I know how much that meant to you, and now you're just up and selling? And what about this estate? You and your father went in together on this, so half is yours."

Why was their mom going on and on? Brad, for one, thought selling was for the best after all the heartache Neil and Candy had been through about that resort. The property had been at the heart of their problems, but not all of them. Brad knew it was also the choices Neil had made, thinking he knew what was best for his wife, for his family. This house, this estate, Brad was sure Neil had spoken to his dad about buying him out.

"It's time to close that door, time for Neil and me to move on with our future," Candy said, gesturing softly with her hand, taking in her husband as if she was speaking for him. And damn if Neil didn't look proud of her. "Neil and I have talked about this, and it's what he wants."

It was quiet for a moment as Candy glanced down at the table. Maybe she thought she'd said too much. Brad couldn't get over the change in her, though. She was much more confident than the scared young woman Neil had brought to the ranch before he married her.

"And what is it you want, Candy?" Brad asked. He could feel Emily tighten beside him, her arm around his waist, but he also knew she had to be thinking the same thing.

Candy flicked her gaze across the table to Neil as a shy

smile touched her lips. She glanced up at Brad then. Brad could also feel the exact moment Neil turned his way, and the look his brother gave him let him know he was treading a fine line, but then, Brad couldn't help being a little protective of Candy after the hurdles Neil had flung at her time and again. She'd hung in there even though, before his mom's stroke, Brad had known she was considering leaving his brother for good.

"I want my family, Brad. I want to go home." She took a breath as she looked over at Neil again. "The resort was important to you, including your life wheeling and dealing with investors and all the high-class people who visited. I was never comfortable with it. I want just a family, just you."

"And that's what we're going to have," Neil said.

"I see," Becky said. "Well, then I guess that settles it. We'll stay here, hang around the pool. Brad, Neil, Jed, you take your father and the kids out." His mom picked up her fork as if everything she'd just heard made absolute sense.

Brad could see his mom had her mind set on spending time with their wives. Maybe it was a good thing, but as he glanced out the open French doors, taking in Katy, Becky, and Trevor, with a bouncing two-year-old Christopher and Danny now pushing away from the table to race around, over to Neil's baby and Cat, he wondered how many vehicles they'd have to take.

CHAPTER

Ten

Watching her sons load up two vehicles, organize car seats, and then get out and move to another vehicle was almost comical. However, Becky was also watching her daughter-in-laws, particularly Diana, who seemed to worry more than any of the women about where the men were going with her children. She had never seen this sort of fear and uncertainty in Diana before. Even Jed had a moment where he rested his hand on her cheek, sliding it into her hair to hold her, before saying something that Diana seemed to accept.

"Are you all right?" Candy was beside her, watching the men, touching Becky's back and rubbing. They stood on the stone deck at the front door.

Becky took in Emily, who had her head shoved in the backseat of Neil's SUV, where her youngest was buckled. Becky couldn't be prouder of the choices her sons had made, the mothers of her grandchildren—she couldn't have picked any better. "Diana seems shaken, more than usual. Have you talked with her?"

Candy waved to her husband as he slid behind the wheel. "Not much. She was so busy looking after her two little ones. She seemed unusually distracted."

"Hmm. I think this is good that the men are off with the kids. That way, we can catch up."

Jed climbed in with Neil, while Brad would drive the minivan. Emily walked over to Diana where she stood in the middle of the large, round concrete driveway past where the Lincoln Rodney drove was parked. She slipped her arm around Diana's waist, and the two started walking back to the house. Diana's mouth was tight. Whatever Emily said to her, she nodded.

"Well, what do you say we all get our swimsuits on and meet at the pool in back?" Becky said. No one replied. Could the women be any less interested? "Come on, you three. This is supposed to be fun. How often do you get a break? I can remember raising my boys, and there wasn't a time I ever got to myself. I ran the house, the ranch… I was always on and would have killed for a day to myself. I never had a mother in-law or sisters, so it was just Rodney and me. My mom and dad would visit sometimes, but it's not the same."

Becky started into the house first and looked up at the iron railing and what felt like a mile of stairs. "Candy, would you mind running upstairs to my room? My black swimsuit is in the top dresser drawer. If you bring it down, I'll get changed in the downstairs bathroom."

"Are you sure? We can help you upstairs," Emily said. Diana said nothing as she looked at the stairs and then Becky.

"Honestly, if I go up those stairs and back down again, it will wear me out," Becky said. "Don't you dare tell your father or my sons," she added.

Candy appeared amused. After all, she'd been here and

seen Neil and Rodney firsthand over all the days following the stroke. It just went with the territory: a Friessen man and his overprotectiveness and worry.

"But you shouldn't overdo it," Emily said, then seemed to think better of it. "Sorry, I guess you hear enough of that.

"Oh, yes, but don't worry. I'll push myself as hard as I need to without breaking me," Becky replied. She watched as her three daughter-in-laws went up the stairs, and she realized this was the first time the four of them had ever had a girls' afternoon of fun with no kids. "Well, we better do this more," she said out loud and then started to the back of the house.

BECKY WAS TALKING with Ana in the kitchen when Candy showed up first in her green bikini with a cotton swimsuit cover wrapped around her waist. She looked amazing, and, at one time, Becky'd had a figure just as amazing. Before she had children, of course. "Wow. That's a great color on you. Once upon a time, I could wear a bikini."

"Me, too. I'm so jealous," Emily said, following her. She wore a wide-brimmed sunhat and a purple and white one piece with a swimsuit cover thrown overtop.

"Em, don't kid yourself. You have a great figure. You should wear one!" Candy said as she handed the swimsuit to Becky.

"No, I couldn't. Having kids left me just a little soft in places a bikini can't hide."

Becky could hear flip flops in the hall right before Diana appeared in a pink bikini top and a black and white skirt. She was carrying a bottle of sunscreen and a towel.

"Oh, I forgot the sunscreen! I'm going to burn if I'm not careful," Emily said.

"You can use mine." Diana stopped. "But I forgot to pack a hat, one of many things missing."

"Not to worry, Diana," Becky said. "Whatever you forgot, we probably have two of. Candy can grab you one. Carlos put some umbrellas up for us so we're out of the sun. I'll get changed and meet you girls out there." She started to the bathroom.

"Can I help you get changed?" Candy asked.

"How about you three go out, and if I need help I'll call you," she replied. She was glad they didn't push, although Candy was the last to leave, watching her for a moment, her expression guarded, before finally turning and following Diana and Emily out to the pool.

She wondered for a moment about what was going through her dark-haired daughter-in-law's head. Well, if anything, the next few hours would give them a chance to find out—maybe. At times, Candy could close herself off to a place where no one could reach her.

"Oh, yes, his way of dealing with the situation is throwing me down for a good old-fashioned shagging," Emily said before sipping on her second glass of wine.

Becky couldn't help smiling as Diana and Candy both laughed. Evidently, Jed and Neil weren't that different from their elder brother. But then, Rodney had kept her happy for many, many years.

Diana covered her wine glass when Candy went to refill it. "No, one's good for me. Besides, I'm not much of a drinker, and I'm feeling a little lightheaded now. And, uh…"

For a moment, she appeared so sad. Becky was lying in one of the loungers, a towel over her legs, holding the small glass of wine she'd insisted Candy pour her. It was a good idea, she thought, to have Ana bring out the wine, cheese, crackers, and fruit on the small table beside them. Candy and Diana were sitting in two of the lounge chairs, and Emily was in the other lounger. For the first time since she'd been here, she seemed absolutely relaxed.

"What is it?" Candy asked, putting the wine bottle down on the table after refilling her own glass.

"My mother was a drinker, a partier. Always out looking for a good time. She'd close the bar down every night, the drugs, the men. Always drunk." Diana waved her hand in front of her face as if to wipe the memory away.

"Diana, you're not your mother," Becky said. She could see now what Jed was talking about.

"I know," she said, staring down at her empty glass, but the way she said it was as if she didn't really believe it.

Emily's expression was filled with concern as she stared at Diana. She opened her mouth to say something and then stopped.

"You had it pretty bad, Diana," Becky said. "You were never allowed to be a child. You had to be the parent instead. It's unforgivable, any parent doing that to their child…and Jed said you had a baby sister who died." Becky knew there had to be way more aside from the little bit Jed had shared. Diana never talked of her past. She couldn't blame her.

Diana was looking down, and a tear fell to her lap. The silence had gone from happiness to sorrow in a matter of seconds. When Diana glanced back up, she didn't try to hide her pain. Her eyes were red and glossy with tears. "Do you know, when my mother showed up, she had no idea Louisa had died? I said to myself, how could she not know? She never asked about her, where she was buried, nothing. So I said to her, 'You know Louisa died the night you were arrested,' and do you know what she said?"

Becky knew it wasn't a question. Candy was rubbing her hand over Diana's shoulder and back, sitting closer to her to let her know she was there and watching Diana with the same concern they all shared.

Diana swiped at her eyes. "She just waved her hand in the air, her expression that same annoyed look she'd give me time and again as a kid when she had other things on her mind and I was annoying her. And then she said, 'I know that, of course I do. Those damn cops, ignoring my baby like that.' And then, in the next breath, she smiled and said it was probably just as well, as Louisa wasn't quite right. But then, my mother made her that way. As I look back, I can see she probably had fetal alcohol syndrome. The signs were there, but there was no help for her, or for us, being the daughters of Faye Claremont."

Diana was staring into her empty wine glass, running her fingers around the rim. "I could never figure out why she chose booze and drugs over her children. How could a mother do that?"

"Oh, Diana, a real mother would never choose anything over her children," Becky said. "But you can't change how people are. Your mother wasn't a mother, and you need to accept that. Is that why you've been fretting about your boys?"

"I don't know, I guess. It rattled me when she showed up, and when she left, I started questioning everything."

"What were you questioning?" Emily asked.

"She said she wanted to make amends, that she was my mother and I had to love her because of that. That she made mistakes, but she's different now. The whole time, I was holding Christopher. He was so heavy, and he wanted down, but I was so scared. I was holding him tight to keep all her badness away from him. I didn't want any of what I survived to come into his life or Danny's. But she just stood there. I was staring at her, and my heart was hammering. She looked older, but she still had the same red hair, and her eyes…they were mine. I started putting it all together in that moment. I couldn't get my tongue to move, as my throat had thickened and started to close up. It took every-thing in me just to breathe as all the memories flashed back of the night we fled, the night Andy burned us out."

"Andy burned you out?" Candy appeared stunned as she stared at Becky. She didn't know the whole story, of course. Becky didn't, either, other than the bits and pieces her son had told her. Emily looked down at her glass, but she didn't appear too surprised.

"He was a different person then, following his daddy," Diana said. "We've all done things we wish we could go back and do differently. Just having the wisdom to see it then as we do now with clear eyes and not as some fantasy would be a gift. But unfortunately we can't. We can only do what we can today, in this moment."

"I can't imagine, Diana, what you went through, and then to have your mother show up again…" Emily pulled up her knees and was leaning forward. "Brad told me long ago. I always wondered about Andy. There was always this tension as if he didn't quite fit. But he's estranged from his family, his father, his mother." Emily was looking to Diana, Candy, and then Becky as if she wasn't entirely sure.

"He is," Diana said. "Time has a way of changing a person. Andy was…a big part of my past, but we moved past what happened after Jed and I married. He's been a big part of helping Jed and me. It's different now, and I don't see him anymore as that young man I worshipped, whose daddy used my mother as his plaything. He was a boy who did what his father asked. No, he's different. I know he's sorry, and he, too, has grown up."

"Yes, he did," Becky said. "I'm proud of him, the way he stood up to his no-good father and mother and married that young girl who needed help. He did right by her, by his children. We aren't our parents, Diana. You see that in Andy: He's not his father, and you're not your mother."

"I know. Jed keeps telling me the same thing, and I know he's irritated with me for not believing it. Even though I tell my head over and over, the problem is my heart doesn't get the same message. I can't make myself believe it, but I keep saying it."

"So what did you do, Diana? You asked her to leave? Is she coming back?" Emily slid her half-full wine glass onto the table between them.

"No, I couldn't say anything. Jed appeared. I saw him walking to the house from the barn, and I could tell he was trying to figure out who was here. He must have seen I was upset, because when he saw me holding Christopher and Danny came running out of the barn, Jed called out to him to go back inside. He asked me who she was—and what was my mother doing this entire time but eyeing him up in a way that was entirely inappropriate? What, did she think my husband would even consider her? I was embarrassed, Jed had to know.

"I still couldn't speak, and Jed was watching me when my mother said proudly, 'Why, I'm Diana's mother!' And then she started going on and on about how proud she was of me and that she was responsible for me being such a good girl, and then she went on about how I took after her. 'Like mother like daughter,' she said. I wanted to cry. Then Danny came running from the barn and up the steps and asked who the pretty lady was. Of course, my mother smiled and blurted out that she was my mother, his grandmother, but he couldn't call her that because she wasn't that old. Of course she wouldn't want that.

"Jed told me to take Danny and Christopher in the house, and then he closed the door behind us. I tried to pull it together, and Danny could tell something was wrong, but I tried to pretend and do something useful like make lunch, only I cut my finger slicing an apple. Then Jed walked in as I heard her car pulling away. I couldn't help worrying about what he thought of me. You know when you get that irrational thought in your head that you're not good enough for someone?"

Becky's heart squeezed as she listened to the agony Diana was struggling with. This was far worse than Jed had mentioned. She wondered if her son really understood how tormented his wife was.

"Oh, Diana, please don't think that," Emily said. She always tried to make everyone feel better. Candy tucked Diana's short hair behind her ears, touching the ends of her hair.

"I tried, but I was so worried, and I was shaking when Jed stepped closer to me. I was afraid, maybe of what he would say to me. But then he put his arms around me and pulled me close, and I just held on as he rubbed my back and held me, and then I started shaking, this uncontrollable shake that had my teeth chattering. It was bad. I couldn't cry, I was frozen. I could hear Jed talking to the boys, but I couldn't understand what he was saying as I just stayed there in his arms. I fisted my hands in his shirt—I got blood on it—and he just kept kissing me here." Diana touched the side of her head and shut her eyes as if reliving the memory.

"What did Jed tell your mother, Diana?" Becky needed to know that her son was all over this, even though she believed he was.

"He told her to leave and never come back. That was all he told me." She leaned forward and put the empty wine glass on the table, then stood up, stepping out of her skirt and showing her pink bikini bottoms. "I'm going for a swim," she said. And then she walked away to the steps of the pool and waded in.

Candy and Emily both looked from Diana to Becky. The shock on their faces said it all. They, too, were at a loss about what to say or do.

Twelve

"Well, I hope the women had a good time," Jed said. He had the passenger window open after Neil shut off the air conditioning. He hated air conditioning and didn't believe it was good for the kids to have that cold air blowing on them. Jed glanced back to his two boys, fast asleep, and Michael, who also had his eyes closed in his baby seat, sucking on his soother.

Neil was following Brad, who was ahead of them in the minivan after spending most of the afternoon at the beach. Neil had taken them to the resort he was selling for lunch, which was a little tense, considering they had seven kids to entertain and keep quiet in a crowded dining room.

"I'm sure they did. Times like these make you appreciate your wife," Neil said. He didn't look his way, but Jed knew he was referring to Danny and Christopher, who hadn't sat still long enough to eat their lunch. They were a handful at times, but then, he and Diana didn't go out to eat often, and it was different when they were at home.

"Diana is a wonderful mother," Jed agreed. "She would

have been the one getting after the boys and making them sit back down."

"Brad's got it easy," Neil said. "But then, he's got Katy, who's on Trevor for him to use his napkin, to stop burping out loud. A little Emily, she is." He smiled.

"Well, Brad is past the diaper and toddler stage. He's got three kids who listen or else. Did you see little Becky's face when he didn't give her a choice on what she was ordering? She wanted macaroni and cheese, and he ordered her the sea bass. Even Dad was surprised by that." Jed chuckled under his breath at the horror on his seven-year-old niece's face when she was served the big piece of fish with shaved carrot on a bed of rice, kale salad on the side. Brad had commented that she needed to broaden her horizons and that he was done with her unwillingness to try anything new. "She really is a picky eater."

"He's tough, but she ate it. She liked it, too, after the first few mouthfuls. Wonder what Emily would have done?" Neil said. Brad's wife was a strong woman, and at times it could appear to someone who didn't know them as if Brad dictated everything, but when you took a closer look, you saw how he truly was a man who'd do anything for his wife and his children. He loved her, he loved his family, and she respected him. Jed understood that respect, as Brad was the big brother who was there for all of them and would always have his back, no matter what.

"Are you sure about selling that resort?" Jed said. He wondered what Neil would do now, as building that resort had been his dream. Neil had always been go big or go home, and now, with selling the property and moving to some rural ranch with his wife and kids, it didn't seem as if Neil would be happy.

"Yeah, I am." He stared straight ahead through the windshield, following Brad down the highway back to the estate. He had sunglasses covering his eyes, and at times Neil could be unreadable.

"Do you think you can be satisfied with that? I mean, Neil, you've always been in a class beyond the rest of us. You're all about bigger." Jed gestured out at the countryside.

At least that lightened Neil's mood just a bit. He flashed a cocky smile. "Yeah, well, things change, Jed. You figure out what's really important, and you go with it. None of us are who we were." He glanced up in the rearview mirror, looking back on the sleeping kids. Cat was in the minivan with Brad. Neil's adopted daughter and Brad's youngest, Becky, were inseparable.

"You surprise me sometimes," Jed said. He did, at times, have trouble figuring out what made Neil tick. He was the charmer in the family, the best friend to his wife, the brother he'd asked to step in if something happened to him, to look after his wife and his kids. And Neil would, without question.

"Maybe I surprise myself," Neil replied. "But, you know, you decide what's really important and weigh it. Yes, I would love to have my resort and be the biggest and the best in the world, but Candy can't do that life. Oh, she'd do it for me. She'd make herself become part of that world, but it would kill her a little bit every day. She wants smaller, quiet, and I can do that for her. What I can't do is live without Candy, and when you realize the power of that, nothing else matters. It's my wife, our kids. And who knows what I can start once I sell everything here and go back to Hoquiam, to our small place?"

Jed snorted. *He* had a small place, at a thousand square feet. Yes, he had expanded onto the house, adding another six hundred feet of family room and a bigger bedroom to the fixer-upper that he'd bought at auction. But he didn't need or want anything huge and massive and expensive. "Your idea of small and mine are two different things. I haven't seen your small place, but I know the house you bought, and it's twice the size of mine—and oceanfront, too. There's nothing small about your place." He paused. "Does Candy know you're settling for her?"

Neil glanced his way and back to the road, shaking his head. "You don't get it, Jed. I screwed up in a way that is unforgivable. If Candy had done what I did to her, I don't think I could have forgiven her. Yet her heart is so big, and her love is endless. She forgave me. I'm rebuilding her trust in me, and I'll be dammed if I don't do everything I can to earn every ounce of her trust back. I almost lost her. If Mom hadn't had her stroke and forced us all to come back here, I guarantee you I may not have gotten my wife back. I swore I'd do anything if I got a second chance, and every day I'm mindful of my wife and what she wants, what she needs. Anything I decide or choose now is with her first in mind."

Jed was surprised. A humbled Neil was not what he'd expected. "I see that you really mean it."

"Yeah, I really mean it. Don't you dare doubt that, little brother."

When they pulled in to the large circular driveway, Jed stepped out of Neil's SUV. It was so light and bright from the hot afternoon sun. The sky down here had a blueness that was sharper and brighter than anything he saw back at home. He lifted Danny from his car seat, his son rubbing his eyes and grabbing Jed's leg as if unsure of where they were.

"Jed?" his mother called from the doorway. Brad and his dad stepped out of the minivan, the kids all piling out behind them.

Jed unbuckled Christopher, who was still fast asleep,

and lifted him out so he could rest his head on his shoulder. His mom looked upset about something. His dad was already at the door, Brad right behind, and both were listening to something his mom was saying.

Jed started to the door, reaching for Danny's hand when Neil came around carrying Michael, who was now awake and rubbing his tired eyes. His dad and Brad turned when he and Neil approached, and he didn't like the concern in their expressions.

"Jed, I'll take Christopher," Brad said, reaching for him. Of course, now Jed couldn't help wondering what was up. "Come on Danny." Brad said taking the kids into the house. Neil stopped beside him.

"What's going on?" Jed said. He didn't like the way his mom and dad looked at each other.

"It's Diana. I'm worried about her, and I think you need to be, too," Becky said.

He didn't like what he was hearing. For his mom to say how worried she was about his wife, he knew it had to be bad, because there was one thing about his mom: She didn't turn things into something they weren't. She didn't worry unnecessarily. She was practical, levelheaded, and was always the one pointing out the positive side of everything.

"What happened?" His mind was going to places he didn't want to go.

"You were right about a lot of things, Jed. Her mother showing up really upset her. I don't know everything that happened to her as a child, and a lot of that is between you and Diana, but I do know, listening to Diana…we heard some things from her, Jed. Your wife is far from okay, and I want to know exactly what you plan to do with the likes of Faye Claremont so she never again contacts your wife."

Jed didn't know what to say to that. Strong arming was

not something his mom ever did, and for a minute he realized what his mom was asking of him.

"I think maybe it's time we have a family meeting." Neil put his hand on his shoulder and squeezed.

"She's my wife, Neil. I'll handle whatever needs to be done."

"Of course, Jed," Becky said. "But Diana is family. She's our family, part of this family, and there's a time when we all need to stand together. Your brother is right. It's time we have a family meeting."

Whatever was going through his mom's head, Jed wasn't entirely sure he was comfortable with it. His mom looked over at Neil and said, "And it's time we all have a talk about all of us."

Oh no. His mom had only had that look about her two times in his life—and one of them was the time Brad, Neil, and him were brought home in the back of the sheriff's car. That was a moment in time he'd never forget. However well meaning his mother was, there was one thing she never did, and that was interfere in his marriage. Whatever was going on in her head, he wasn't sure he was going to like it.

Thirteen

Neil watched as his brother went into the house. Neil didn't know what to make of this, of Diana. He liked Diana and Emily. They were not only his brothers' wives, they were his friends, his sisters. He glanced at his mom, who was staring at him with a determination he wasn't sure he liked.

"Where's Candy?" he said.

"Out back with Emily, by the pool," she replied. It was then he noticed his mom was in sandals and a swimsuit cover that draped to her knees. "Diana is in the pool still, or that's where she was when I went into the kitchen and heard you drive in. I think you should talk to her, too. Jed's her husband, but I know you all look out for one another and for the mothers of my grandkids."

"Maybe you should just let Jed talk to Diana," Rodney said. He appeared a little uncomfortable, and Neil wasn't sure why.

"Sometimes, Rodney, we need someone else to talk to us. You know that. We wouldn't be where we are if we didn't."

Neil wasn't sure what to make of what his mom had said. His dad didn't look too willing to share, either. Michael started to fuss in his arms, rubbing his eyes. Neil could feel that his bottom was wet. "I'm going to get this guy changed," he said.

He was halfway up the stairs when he noticed his mom and dad walking together. His dad was watching his mom, his hand ready to take her arm in case she needed it. He couldn't put his finger on it, but there was something going on.

After changing the baby and putting him in a dry onesie, he stopped in the kitchen long enough to warm up a bottle. Michael grabbed for it and leaned back in Neil's arms as he sucked on the warm milk. He stepped outside and took in Diana at the other end of the pool, leaning with her arms on the edge, Jed in front of her, crouched down, talking to her. Brad was sitting on the lounge chair with Emily, her legs resting on his lap. He still had Christopher, who was fast asleep, his head on Brad's shoulder. Danny was with Becky and Cat, and Trevor and Katy were sitting together at a picnic table eating popsicles.

"Can I get you something, Mr. Neil?" Ana appeared beside him, coming from the house, carrying a tray with a bowl of potato chips, stacked plastic cups, and a jug of juice.

"No, I'm good. Is that for the kids?" he asked, reaching in and helping himself to a chip.

"Yes, it is. It's so good to have all your family here. It's good for Mrs. Friessen," Ana replied. She was so calm, and he'd miss her and Carlos, her husband, who'd been here working at the estate since he and his father had bought the land and moved down here. After building this huge estate and starting the ranch, the herd of cattle at the other end of the ten-thousand-acre property, well, they were almost like family.

"Have you seen my wife?" he asked.

"I think she went down to the stables," Ana said. "Oh, and dinner. Mrs. Friessen wanted to have a barbecue tonight. Carlos is going to start the grill soon."

Neil watched as Ana made her way over to the kids. He'd forgotten how much Ana liked kids, and the kids seemed overjoyed by the treats. Neil walked across the concrete deck around the pool. Brad glanced up first, and Neil noticed the wine bottle and empty glasses on the table beside Emily.

"Did you drink that whole thing?" he teased.

Emily glanced up at him under her wide-brimmed hat. Brad was rubbing her bare legs. "No, but I had enough," she said. She wasn't smiling, and neither was Brad.

"Everything okay over there?" He gestured with his chin to the edge of the pool where Diana and Jed were. Whatever Jed said, Diana had pulled herself out of the pool. Jed wrapped a towel around her. They walked around the other side of the pool, away from everyone, as if Jed knew Diana needed space. They slipped through the French doors to the dining room.

Emily was watching them walk away, and her expression was similar to his mom's. "Oh, I hope so."

"Em was just filling me in," Brad said. "I think Mom is right. We need to have a family meeting. Diana needs to know who her family is: us. I don't like seeing her like this, as if she truly believes she's alone."

Neil also wanted a moment to talk one on one with Diana, to really get a bead on where her head was. They'd been through so much together, and he'd seen her at her worst, when she'd almost lost her husband. "I'm pretty sure Mom is going to make sure that happens. She's determined. Can't say I've quite seen her like this. She's always been the one telling us not to interfere, and here she is." Neil really didn't know what to make of this situation right now—or what his mother wanted to say. "I'm going to wander over to the stables and find my wife."

Brad was helping Emily up from the lounger when he walked away. He spotted Candy at the end of the path where the small corral was shaded by trees, the one he'd built for her horse and donkey after the storm. She was brushing her horse, Sable, a smoky gray Azteca. The young donkey Candy had rescued, Ambrose, was rubbing his face against her butt. She wore a cotton wrap around her waist and a green bikini top. There wasn't much to it, but then, Neil had bought it for her, one of many he loved seeing her in. She was wearing an old pair of sneakers on her feet, and her hair was knotted in a messy bun on top of her hair. Absolutely gorgeous.

"Well, that's quite a sight."

She glanced up. There was a smudge of dirt on her cheek. "Hey, I didn't know you were back." She strode over to the rail where Neil leaned with Michael in his arms, drinking his bottle. Candy appeared conflicted before leaning in and kissing Neil. She touched Michael's head, rubbing the soft dark hair, and then kissed him, too. Michael grunted in appreciation as he continued sucking on his bottle.

"So how was your afternoon out? What did you do?"

"Oh, went to the beach, watched Jed race after his two boys. Went for lunch, watched Jed come close to losing it because Danny and Christopher wouldn't sit still. Brad actually scooped up Danny after we were all getting tired of the boys' antsy-pantsy behavior, and he made Christopher sit on his lap. He discovered right quick that he wasn't Dad!"

Candy didn't smile. She seemed so distracted. "Your cousin is still coming?"

The way she said it bothered Neil. Candy liked Andy and Laura. After all, she'd been there when they were fighting to save their little boy's life while he fought his leukemia.

"Yes, they are. With Laura pregnant again, I know he was worried and wanted to be sure it was okay for her to travel. As far as I know, they're still flying in. Should be here tomorrow."

Candy nodded, but she wore a look he didn't like, the same one she'd had for him not too long ago. It was an expression he never wanted to see again. "You've never really told me that much about your cousin, but I'm not sure I like the picture that was painted of him today."

Oh no! What the hell had the other women said? He could only imagine. Sometimes, hearing about the past wasn't a good thing, because that wasn't who Andy was now. "Candy, before you heard what you did today, what did you think about my cousin?"

She seemed startled and frowned, and he could see her thinking. "In the beginning, he terrified me. Actually, all your family did. But your cousin…there was something about the way he watched people that was so hard. After spending time with Andy and Laura and their babies, though—he's an amazing father, and I saw a man who would do anything for his children, for Laura. I found it odd how he married someone so young, and odder still when I heard how he met Laura. She was barely nineteen, and he did it to save her son when he was taken away from her because she was homeless. It's quite a story, and my respect grew for him.

"I wasn't always sure he loved her, but watching them together trying to save Gabriel, and how Andy loved her illegitimate little boy so much that he didn't believe for a moment he wasn't his, it was inspiring. I had a new respect for Andy. Talking with him after, I wasn't so scared, and I realized he was just like all of us. But now, after hearing what he did to Diana as a kid…she was just a young, innocent child, Neil!"

He had to reach out and touch her face, her shoulder. He could feel the tension and how twisted up she was feeling. "We all have something in our past. I'm no different. Look at me. If I could go back and undo everything I did…" He paused, because Michael had come out of one of the biggest lies he'd ever created. Maybe she knew, as she flushed and then glanced lovingly down on their son.

"I know what you're saying, Neil." She didn't say anything else as she ran her hand over their baby's head again. "But Andy, what he did to Diana, she was just a kid. She wasn't her mother. I don't know how I feel or how I can be in the same room with him now, knowing what he did."

How could he make her understand that was another time? They'd all moved past it. So had Diana, until Faye showed up and brought back all those horrible memories. "I'm going to talk to Diana," he said.

Candy rested her hands on the corral rail. "Oh?"

"She's my friend, she's Jed's wife, she's a sister to me. Sometimes it helps having someone to talk to who isn't your husband."

She wouldn't look at him as she nodded. "You're probably right. I should know that, since I…" She stopped talking as if she realized she shouldn't say any more.

"You what? Come on, Candy. I wish you would just tell me."

When she looked at him this time, her expression was

filled with regret. "I don't want to hurt you, and it doesn't matter now."

Maybe it was the way he waited for her that made her finally shrug and say, "I understand because I had Brad to talk to, and he helped—but it was your father and mother who convinced me to stay."

Fourteen

Dinner was quieter than usual. All the adults sat in the comfortable dining room, and the chatter from the kids could be heard through the open French doors. The lights were dimmed on the crystal chandelier, and the green and white trim in this private room added to the elegance. Brad felt it had Neil written all over it. Although his mom had great taste, Neil had always been the one who wanted that little bit more.

The food, as usual, was abundant. The steaks were cooked to perfection, and the corn was juicy, with baked potatoes and a creamy Caesar salad to start. Although everyone was talking and the kids were having so much fun, a noticeable tension hung in the air. Diana hadn't said a word all night.

"After dinner, when the kids are in bed, I want to have a family meeting," Becky said. "In the living room. I think it's past time we all came together and talked."

Everyone looked up. Candy and Diana appeared startled. Jed was shaking his head, but he didn't say anything. Emily looked to Brad, and he knew his wife was divided on the meeting. However, she did agree with him that Diana needed to know she had a family already, those who were in her corner, who loved her. She had to know she wouldn't have to go through anything alone ever again. He noticed Candy's puzzled expression as she glanced over at Neil, and, of course, Brad could tell by his expression that he'd forgotten to mention it to Candy.

"What's going on?" she whispered to Neil, not quietly enough.

"I'll tell you later." He put his arm over her bare shoulder, rubbing the strap of the light blue sundress she'd donned for dinner. She had gold hoops in her ears, and her long dark hair shone like silk as it hung straight down her back. She was stunning, and Brad hoped yet to pull Candy aside and talk to her, make sure everything was good between her and Neil. "You done?" Neil said to Brad from where he sat across the table.

Of course. It was way too much food, even though he'd polished off the juicy piece of sirloin and done his share of making a dent in the feast. He shoved his plate back with his fingers. "Yeah," he said, putting his arm around the back of Emily's chair.

"If you'll excuse us for a minute, I need to have a chat with my big brother," Neil said, sliding his chair back and putting his napkin on his plate. He touched Candy's shoulder, and her expression appeared startled. Maybe she had some idea what this was about.

"I also want to talk about our anniversary," Becky said, looking over at him.

Brad didn't know why she was looking to him. She should've been talking to Neil, who loved planning events, or even Emily, Diana and Candy. Unless he needed to pick something up or move something, Brad wasn't too interested in playing any part in the planning process.

"Don't look so worried, Brad," his mom added. Emily chuckled beside him.

"I'm not worried, Mom, I'm just not sure what's to discuss. Just tell me where and when to show up. Anything else, you can talk to my lovely wife."

Emily actually reached up and lightly smacked his arm. There were a few chuckles as he followed Neil out of the dining room.

"So what's going on, Neil?" Brad followed his brother into the kitchen. Ana wandered in, carrying dirty plates with half-eaten food, which had to be from the kids.

"Let's go in the living room, where it's quiet." The way Neil said it sounded as if he had a bone or two to pick with him.

Neil didn't sit down but stood in front of the large fire-place. He rested one hand on the stone mantel and ran his other over the beard he was starting to grow. With his longish, naturally wavy hair, he was starting to resemble a pirate.

"What's so important you needed to pull me out, Neil?" Brad wandered down the two wide steps into the living room and around the sofa. He stopped in front of Neil and crossed his arms.

"What did you talk to my wife about?" Neil said.

He actually had to look away as he tried to figure out what his brother was talking about. "Suppose you tell me what's going on and maybe give me a little more information."

"Brad, did you or did you not talk to my wife and be a shoulder for her to lean on when we had our problems?"

"Where's this coming from, Neil?"

The dark look Neil leveled on him was far from reason-able. "Don't play games, Brad. Just answer me, please."

"Yes, I talked to Candy. If you recall, I was there when

she found out what you did and how you lied about Michael. I saw the letter. You were on the other side of the country, remember? I saw how far apart you were. She wasn't going to talk to you or listen to you. You know that." He gestured between them. "Why are we rehashing this? You two seem as if you worked things out."

Neil appeared frustrated and tired at the same time. "We have. I mean, we're working things out. And I know you were there. I thought I had lost her. I didn't know what to do to win her back."

"It's not about winning, Neil. But yeah, you're right, she had one foot out the door. I don't know how much talking to me helped, but it seems as if you two are working things out. She doesn't look like a woman about to leave her husband, not like she was."

"No, we've come a long ways. I've done everything I can to win back her trust. I can't do anything more than I've already done."

"I don't understand, Neil, why you're upset that I spoke with Candy. She needed to know she was a part of our family, that she has someone to talk to. I'm pretty sure she was feeling alone."

He wasn't sure Neil agreed, but then, he'd seen the possessive side of Neil that wanted to control everything Candy did. It was quite a transformation happening in his brother, having to let go of so much control.

"You're not going to ask me what we talked about?" Brad said. He'd been waiting for that demand from Neil, but his brother just watched him as if waging a mental war.

He nodded. "No, as much as I want to know, I won't ask. I want her to tell me. I can't do that to her. We've come too far. She'd be really mad."

"Well, I'm impressed, Neil. Maybe there is hope for

you." Brad could see how hard his brother was trying. He still wanted to talk to Candy at some point during his stay, just to make sure he was reading the situation correctly.

"Answer me this: Would you have told me if I asked?"

It was the one question he didn't want his brother asking, because if it had been him, he'd have expected his brother to come clean and tell him. But everything wasn't so black and white. "No, I wouldn't have."

"And if it was Emily?"

He let out a sharp laugh and shook his head. "You're an asshole. Of course I'd expect you to tell me, but it's not the same. Emily wouldn't keep something like that from me. We share everything. It's different with us."

"Really, you're so sure about that, are you? She tells you everything?"

Where was he going with this? Neil obviously knew he'd zeroed in on his weakness, and he didn't appreciate what his brother was implying. After all, Emily would tell him if something was wrong, right?

CHAPTER

Fifteen

Whatever was going on with Brad and Neil was obviously something significant, as they both returned to the dining room pensive. Well, Brad was moody, and the way he glanced down at his wife, watching her as if there was something he needed to speak with her about, made Becky wonder what had brought this on. Then there was brooding Neil, who put his arm around Candy and just listened quietly to the conversation.

For the anniversary, she had no input at all from her family, and Neil, the executive who needed to organize everything, seemed more comfortable sitting back and doing nothing. Diana, Emily, and Candy volunteered to do anything she needed help with, but they had no ideas other than a nice dinner after the ceremony Becky had planned. She wanted to snap her fingers at their glumness. When she glanced over at Rodney, she saw that he, too, had noticed the change in demeanor in their kids. When everyone got up from the table, Diana, Emily, and Neil went outside to check on the kids. Wherever Candy wandered off to, Becky wasn't sure. Both Jed and Brad had disappeared.

It was almost nine when Jed stuck his head into the living room, where Becky was seated in the leather chair with her feet resting on the ottoman. She was alone, waiting for her family. "You seen Diana, Mom?" Jed asked.

"Last I saw, she was dragging your youngest up the stairs for a bath, and he was arguing that he wasn't tired and didn't want to get ready for bed."

"Oh, that's just Christopher. He's got a stubborn streak just like his mother." Jed laughed and started down the steps, then rested his hands on the back of the sofa. Becky noticed he'd changed into blue jeans and those ratty cowboy boots she still couldn't believe he'd worn down to Cancun. Once a cowboy, always a cowboy, she supposed. But at least he had on a nice white dress shirt.

"I'm sure Christopher takes more after you than Diana. You were the most stubborn of all my children."

He quirked an eyebrow and frowned, then snorted. "I think not. The stubborn one, I'm sure, is Neil. I'm the easy one."

She had to smile. Her three boys were so alike in a lot of ways but miles apart in their individuality. "Sit down, Jed."

Jed glanced behind him and around the room. "Where's Dad?" He sat on the ottoman beside Becky's feet.

"He's helping Carlos move the grill back to the shed. He'll be back soon."

Jed nodded. He didn't say anything else as he looked around. He was her quiet, moody boy who could hold on to something and not say a word for days. He was her deep thinker and could be such a pain in the ass when he believed in something.

"Tell me how things are at home on your little ranch," she said.

Jed was never one to really share what was going on in his struggle to make it on his own, starting a small ranch from nothing, taking people on trail rides and weekend pack trips into the mountains on horseback. He'd even started therapeutic riding for special needs children, which had been one of Diana's ideas. Becky really believed this was because of the loss of her baby sister. She was trying to help all the Louisas in the world.

"Everything's good, Mom."

"Do you think you could elaborate a little more, Jed? Sometimes getting anything out of you is similar to pulling teeth."

He laughed softly. "Fine. I have a busy summer booked, lots of people who've paid for some overnight camping trips on horseback. A few big groups, and I have twelve special needs kids riding. I had to stop taking kids until I can hire more help. We have a waitlist. So stop worrying, Mom. Everything's going good."

"And what about Diana? Any hint of her wanting to take up the law again? I mean, she has a law degree and she put everything aside for you. Maybe she needs to practice part time. It would help her gain back her self-confidence."

Jed was shaking his head. He could be so stubborn, just like his brothers. None of her sons' wives had their own careers. They were so much about family. "No, she needs to be home. She's my wife. I'll look after her. We have children, Mom. I'm not about to have my kids raised by some sitter. I mean, look at you, Mom. You were home and there for us, and I want that for my kids."

"Jed, really, that is pretty selfish, you know. It was different for me. That was what women did. Oh, there were lots that had a career. I went to Berkley, where I met your father. I majored in history. Like, what am I going to do seriously with a history degree? I didn't really think about it then. For me, it was my parents who said I had to have an education, go to college. I didn't know what I wanted to do."

"Well, did you want to work, have a career away from us?" Jed sounded upset.

"Oh Lord, Jed. That's not the point. No, I loved being at home with you and the boys, but I also worked with your dad on the ranch. It's not that it was easy—it wasn't. Being together all the time, we had our struggles. But have you ever asked Diana what she wants?"

He looked away, and she was positive he was about to say yes. Then he appeared to be considering something. "If Diana wanted to be a lawyer still, she'd have said something to me." He had that stubborn streak popping through again.

"Yes, but would you have heard her?"

Jed didn't say anything.

Candy walked into the living room, pulling a cream shawl over her shoulders. "Everything all right?" she asked, looking from Becky to Jed.

"Yes, everything is fine," Becky said as she watched Jed watching her. She could tell he was considering everything she had said.

Neil had just put a sleeping Michael to bed. He was carrying the baby monitor so he could listen in from downstairs. Diana was standing in the doorway to the large children's bedroom where Danny and Christopher were bunked in with Katy and Trevor. Her hand was on the doorframe, and she was just standing there, watching them.

"Are they asleep?" he asked, and she jumped, so lost in thought she hadn't seen or heard Neil come up.

"Danny is even though he argued he wasn't tired." She smiled a forced smile that didn't reach her eyes. No, when Diana smiled, she lit up the room. But there was always a lingering sadness he would catch in the shadow of her eyes. Sometimes, she was lost in thought, unaware anyone was watching her.

"I haven't had a chance to talk with you. Like, is my brother treating you okay and worshipping the ground you walk on like he should be?"

She laughed, and it seemed to ease some of the tension

she was always carrying. She put her arms around his neck and hugged him. "Oh, Neil, I missed you."

He rubbed her back and kissed her cheek. When she pulled away, she had an awkward look unlike the Diana he knew. He couldn't help himself as he reached out and touched the ends of her boyish haircut. It really was unflattering, changing her from the knockout she was to someone who was trying to blend in and go unnoticed. Then he took in her clothes. She'd changed again into a light brown T-shirt and slacks. Bland, ordinary. Where was the Diana he knew? He was almost horrified.

"What's wrong?" she asked, pulling a face as if trying to figure him out.

"I guess I need to ask you the same thing. What is this?" He gestured to her clothes and up to her hair.

She glanced into the kids' room and then stepped away from their door. "You don't like the way I look?"

"Seriously, Diana, have you taken a look in the mirror at yourself?"

Her cheeks pinkened. She didn't say a word.

"Diana, you're a beautiful woman, and that's not just how you look on the outside. It's something that comes from inside of you that takes you from surface beautiful to stunning, and I can see you're trying to take the gift you have and bury it, like you're trying to punish yourself for who you are. Don't do that. You need to love the Diana we all know, the beautiful, brilliant redhead who stole my brother's heart."

She ran her hand over her short hair, pulling on the ends. "I just figured I needed a change."

"Bullshit, Diana. When did you start lying to me?"

She appeared shocked he would talk to her that way. Her bold blue eyes widened. "Neil, I'm not lying."

"You're not telling the truth, either. Your mother shows up and the next day you chop off all your hair."

The sadness appeared again. "I'd forgotten how beautiful she was, but she was older. She's dyed her hair, I'm sure. I didn't realize how much I look like her. I knew I did, but it hurt to see it."

"Just because you look like her doesn't mean you are her." He leaned in, his arms crossed, trying to get through to her.

"I know that, Neil. Really, I do, but seeing her there on my doorstep, I was so afraid." She made a choking sound and then put her palm over her mouth before waving it in the air in front of her as if trying to fan herself.

"What were you scared of?"

"It would sound silly to you."

He was shaking his head and reached out to touch her arm. "Try me." He waited, and he could see her considering.

"Diana?" he urged her again, and when she licked her lips and took a breath, she said, "The first thing I thought of when I saw her was the booze, the pills, the parties, the men. Then there was me being tainted as the daughter of the town whore. I panicked when I thought I'd be ostracized by the townspeople once again. They'd know she was back. Maybe they'd think I'd invited her. Then the way she looked at Jed, as if he was her next conquest, it was the first time I'd ever felt I could actually kill someone. When she said I was just like her, it was as if she planted that seed in me, and I've…" She touched a shaky hand to her mouth.

She was breathing so hard, he could see how twisted up and tormented she was. Everything she'd made right, her mother's sins that she'd paid for, and here she was, right back at the beginning, having to dig her way back to being comfortable with who she was again.

"So you cut your hair off so it wouldn't be like your mother's."

She nodded.

"You're dressing in the most god-awful unflattering clothes so you won't stand out."

Her eyes met his.

"And you're hovering over your children so much that you're almost obsessive with worry because your mother never gave a crap about you. Did I miss anything?"

She lowered her hand. "I had a glass of wine at lunch with Candy and Emily and your mom, and I was having fun, and then I felt guilty, and her words came into my head that I was like her. She was always drinking, partying, having fun."

"Ah, I see. So a glass or two of wine and having some well-deserved fun with the girls and you think you're a drunk, neglecting your children."

Maybe it was the way he said it, but she rolled her eyes. "I told you it would sound silly."

"Hey, how you feel is not silly, but stopping yourself from having fun and living is silly. Stop it, Diana, and put on some nice clothes, would you? You're a beautiful woman. Please be kind to yourself. You deserve it. And I'm going to say this even though you've probably heard it from Jed already: You're not your mother. Don't let her get in your head."

"I'll try, Neil."

"Do more than try. Every time you doubt who you are, you tell yourself how beautiful you are, how loving and kind, and be grateful for what you have. It's in here." He touched her heart. "And here." He touched the side of her head. "And you have amazing children who have a wonderful mother, a family, a husband who loves you, a handsome, dashing brother-in-law…"

She burst out laughing before he could finish. "Oh, Neil, I missed you."

"Good. Shall we adjourn to the living room for the decreed family meeting?" He held out his arm, and Diana slipped her hand on it and walked with him down the stairs.

"By the way, this new look of yours…I've got admit it works for you, Neil." Diana tugged on the beard he'd started now six days ago.

"Really? I was going for the feared rogue pirate look." He loved to hear her laugh.

"Well, drop the 'feared,' but you've got that rogue pirate thing happening."

He stepped off the bottom step, and it took a second for him to realize Diana was no longer smiling. When he looked over, he saw why. Andy Friessen was watching them from where he stood with Jed.

Seventeen

Brad and Emily sat side by side on the sofa, and Candy joined them. Jed was still sitting on the ottoman when they heard a car drive in.

Jed went to the window and looked out.

"Who's here, Jed?" Becky asked. She wasn't about to get up, but she was also waiting for Neil and Diana to both come down so they could have the first ever family meeting.

"It's Andy and Laura." Jed started to the door at the same time that Rodney walked in. Becky listened to the voices outside, and Brad said something to Emily before getting up and going to the door. Emily and Candy wore expressions that were both surprised and uneasy. The last thing she wanted was her nephew, Andy, walking into something with his wife and kids that wasn't comfortable for anyone. Their timing, for that matter, wasn't good.

"I thought they were coming tomorrow?" Candy turned to Emily and asked.

Emily slid around on the sofa and gestured her confusion with her hand. "Well, they're here, and they're family. Maybe this is just as well. Clear up all these ghosts lingering once and for all."

The way Candy was watching her sister-in-law, Becky realized she might not agree.

"Aunt Becky, you look good," Andy said. He looked dashing as ever, tall, dark, and handsome, with his icy blue eyes and short dark hair. He was a well-built man. He could have been her sons' brother, with the same haunting good looks. He kissed her cheek, and she reached up and patted his arm where a tattoo peeked out from under his T-shirt. She pulled it up to have a look at the eagle he'd gotten when he was sixteen. She remembered hearing about it. He had Gabriel beside him. The little dark-haired child had grown. He resembled his mom, with his round cheeks and shy smile, and the way he adored Andy.

Andy let go of Gabriel's hand to pull at the edge of his sleeve. The way he did it, she wondered if he now regretted the tattoo.

"Thank you, Andy. I'm glad you could come. Where's your brood?"

"They're coming. I better go give Laura a hand. Ana is helping her with the twins, but I wanted to say hi."

At times, she wondered if Andy was trying to fit into their family. He seemed so much like an outsider looking in, but he was family even though he was the son of Todd Friessen, Rodney's brother, the man responsible for almost destroying her.

"Gabriel, how are you?" she said to the little boy. Andy ruffled his hair and stepped away.

"Good. Where are Katy and Becky?" he said.

"They're sleeping, honey. It's bedtime for all the kids. Why, we have a nice room ready for you and your mom and dad—and your brother and sister. You must be tired?"

"No, I'm not tired. I want to play," he said, looking shyly at Emily and Candy.

"How about you play in the morning?" Candy said, sliding forward on the sofa. She held out her arms for him to come to her, and he walked around the ottoman.

Becky just happened to glance up, hearing voices, and noticed Diana and Neil coming down the stairs. Jed was speaking with Andy, and whatever he said had changed the atmosphere to tense, especially when Diana spotted him. She'd been smiling one moment at whatever Neil was saying, but she was now back to the sorrowful woman she'd been earlier that day.

Becky reached for her cane to stand up as no one said anything. Both Emily and Candy had noticed, too, the alarm evident in their expressions. Becky was slow, and she cursed not being able to move faster around the chair when a pregnant Laura strode through the front door. Ana was carrying one of the twins, while the other was holding her hand. She stopped, taking in the tension. Anyone would know something was off.

"Is everything all right?" she asked and started toward Diana.

"Yeah, everything's good," Diana said. "Hey, look at you, pregnant again!" She had pulled herself together and pasted a smile on her face, then held out her arms as if she had to remind herself to hug Laura. Rodney was directing Carlos with the luggage up the stairs, and Becky was almost up the steps when she saw Andy step toward Diana.

"So I heard Faye Claremont is back," he said.

"Andy Friessen, leave it to you to bring up the elephant in the room," Becky said as she walked into the mix beside Jed, Neil, Diana, and Andy. Laura was standing beside Diana, and Rodney was looking over everyone.

Laura frowned, turned to Andy, and asked, "Who is Faye Claremont?"

It was a moment of awkward silence, and no one said a thing.

CHAPTER

Eighteen

"How could you?"

Jed could do nothing as he watched his wife pace the living room, her arms crossed over her breasts, even more tightly wound than she had been earlier. What would her breaking point be, he wondered? But then, he realized, she wasn't consumed with sorrow. Her emotions had shifted to blazing anger. Maybe this was better. He'd rather her be ready to fight than sit back and do nothing.

Emily and Candy were still sitting on the sofa, not saying a word, and Neil was standing behind them, his hand resting on the back of it. For the first time, he seemed at a loss for words. At least everyone else had given them some space and was upstairs with Andy, Laura, and the kids, getting them settled for now.

"What would you have me do, Diana, not say anything?"

She threw her hands up in the air and tossed him an irritated look, fire burning in her eyes.

"Yes, Diana, what would you have Jed do?"

Jed hadn't heard Andy come jogging down the steps to join them.

"I don't know, but is this where you threaten me or maybe compare me to my mother?" she snapped, and even Jed wanted to take her aside and shake her.

"Diana," he said in warning.

"It's all right, Jed," Andy said. "No, I wouldn't do that. I thought we were past this, or is there something else going on?"

Of course. There was no way for Andy to have known how tormented his wife was and how Faye showing up had sent Diana into a tailspin.

"Why is your mother back? What does she want?" he asked, but Jed realized Andy was no longer the type of man who would track her down and chase her out of town.

"Apparently to mess with my wife's head. I don't know, but she wants something." Jed was leaning against the fire-place mantel.

"Are you starting this meeting without the rest of us?" his mom called out as she walked with their dad into the living room. Jed watched as his father held his mom as she took the steps one at a time, leaning on her cane.

Then Brad appeared, too. He walked over to Andy and shook his hand, then patted his shoulder. "Good to see you, Andy. How's Montana treating you?"

"Pretty good. How about you, Brad? Things are good?"

"Couldn't be better."

Jed appreciated the break in this building tension. Brad had always been skilled at distracting everyone from awkward things, except when the awkwardness was of his own doing.

"Laura coming down?" Jed asked.

Andy turned and shook his head. "No, she's getting the

kids to bed and going to take a shower. I know she's worn out from traveling all day."

"I'm not that tired, Andy," Laura replied, having appeared at the top of the stairs. She was in a blue paisley maternity top over light blue cotton maternity shorts. She was so tiny that her six-month pregnant belly showed a nice swell. She did stop just short of reaching Andy. Jed didn't like the questions that appeared in her light blue eyes. She and Andy had come so far, overcome so many obstacles—mainly his parents—and had moved their family to another state for a new beginning.

"Laura, you look good," Jed said, picking up on her uncertainty as she took in Diana and then Andy. He wondered if Andy had ever shared any part of the dark past with Laura, about Diana, her mother, and what had really happened.

Laura held her jaw in such a way that Jed could tell she had a few choice words in mind. "You still haven't answered me about who this Faye is who seems to have somehow upset Diana. And you, Andy, I know you know something you haven't shared."

Andy actually held out his hand to Laura, but she didn't take it right away. Her blond hair was curling at the ends and hung just past her shoulders. Her round face was free of makeup, but then, she really didn't need any. She took a step forward and took his hand, and he pulled her to his side. "Where're the kids?" he asked.

"Ana said she'd put them to bed. She thought I should come down. I think she's right."

Jed wondered if Andy agreed, but then, out of all of them, Andy had the most reason to be overly protective of his wife.

"Laura, why don't you sit down?" his mom said from the chair she sat in, his dad perched on the arm beside her.

She gestured to the sofa, where there was an empty spot between Candy and Emily. Brad, meanwhile, had taken the dark wing-backed chair beside the sofa and was taking in everyone.

"Thank you, but I'm fine. Been sitting all day, all this traveling. It feels good to stand up for a bit and move around."

"Faye is my mother, Laura," Diana announced and stopped pacing. "She's not a very nice person."

Laura looked up to Andy, who was staring out into space, not looking at anyone. He appeared to be thinking some heavy thoughts.

"What does she have to do with you, Andy?" Laura asked, and Jed didn't miss the heaviness that came over the room and the glance shared between Diana and Andy.

"Diana's mom was a single mother who liked to party, drink, and do and deal drugs," Becky said, setting the record straight and maybe trying to save Andy some face. "She was the worst of the worst, and I can't imagine having the childhood Diana did."

"And you knew her?" Laura asked Andy.

He'd yet to say anything. Andy was the kind of man who held on to things and spoke when he had something to say. Maybe he was trying to figure out a way to explain what he'd done as a young man who worshipped his no-good father.

"Faye was one of my daddy's playthings," he finally said. "She lived in one of his houses." He frowned and appeared to be considering something still. "You know about my father, my family. Dad has a long string of mistresses. When he was done with them, he'd want them run out of town. That was the way he was, the way he's always been. He controlled the law in North Lakewood for a lot of years, so he could do anything he wanted. I learned at an early age to go in and clean up his mess. Diana's mom went too far, drugging him. I lost it, and we threw them out in the middle of the night and burned the house down. Diana and her sister got caught up in the middle of it. I'm sorry, Diana. We should have helped you."

"Oh, Andy," Laura said, looking over at Diana. This couldn't be good for Laura, the way her expression was filled with remorse.

"This all happened a long time ago, Laura," Becky said, "but Andy has always had to clean up after his daddy. Like you, Diana, with your mother. What the two of you don't realize is no matter what side you two were on, both of you were stuck in an impossible situation."

Everyone looked at Becky. Jed couldn't believe his mom would say that. How could she justify Andy treating Diana, who'd been just a kid, as if she weren't worth anything?

"I can see how all of you can't see it from my perspective," Becky continued, "but, Diana, you had to raise that little sister of yours you lost, tiptoe around your mother, and, I'm betting, look after her instead of her looking after you. You didn't know any other way."

Diana had such a weary look on her face. Jed was able to finally reach over and slide his arm around her, and this time she didn't fight him as she went to him, sliding her own arm around his waist. Her head rested against his shoulder.

"And, Andy, you looked up to Todd. You two did everything together. He was your father. Of course you did as he said, seeing only his side of things."

"Including flexing your muscles for your dad when he asked you to," Jed said. Maybe he was still pissed over what Andy had done, but it seemed as if his mom was letting Andy off the hook, and he wasn't okay with that, considering how he'd treated Diana when she first came back, like a second-class whore.

"Enough, Jed," Diana snapped, and she pressed her hand to his chest. "Yes, having my mother show up the way she did brought everything back from when I was a kid. I thought I had reconciled with the past, but all my fears came back, too, about how hard I'd worked to hold my head up, to show everyone I'm a good person, that I'm not my mother. I don't want to go back to how I was ostracized, or for my kids, our kids, to have the same fate."

"You're not your mother, Diana," Andy said. He shook his head. "If I could go back, I wouldn't have listened. Maybe I would've called for help for you and your sister, I don't know. You know I'm sorry. You're family, Diana. No one is going to treat you badly, or the boys."

"You're right, Andy. No one will treat Diana like that," Jed said—only because, if anyone so much as hinted about causing trouble for his wife or slighting her in any way, it would become his fight, and they'd soon wish they hadn't taken him on. Jed also remembered how Diana had been treated when she'd come back to town as an adult. The townsfolk had a long memory and wouldn't even serve Diana because they thought she was like her mother. Some people forgot, some didn't, and Todd Friessen's hold on that town was strong still. "But you've also left, Andy. In the town, things aren't the same."

"You're right, Jed. We won't be going back, and you know why. I won't allow Laura and my children around my parents. Any hold they may have on that town, they don't have where we are."

Jed and his father both knew just how far Andy's mom would go. Diana did, too. Maybe she remembered, as she looked up at Jed, the night Laura had run away, believing Andy was plotting with his mother to take her children

The night had quieted, and the sun had long since gone down. There were lights surrounding the pool, giving it a romantic feel. Brad should have been dancing with his wife, swimming with her in the salt-water pool, as he watched Neil swimming laps back and forth. Maybe he should join his brother and work off some of his restless energy.

He felt a hand touch his back and glanced down at his wife, who had a light sweater pulled over her shoulders. He lifted his arm, and she went right to his side. "I thought you went to bed," he said. That meeting, which had even his eyes a little misty, leaving him feeling closer to his family than he ever had, had made for an emotional night, and he'd needed to step outside and get some air. Neil must have had the same idea, as he'd changed into his swimsuit and then dived right into the pool without a word.

"No, your mom and dad went up. Candy and Diana are sitting with Laura, talking. I don't know where Jed and Andy went. It's as if everyone scattered."

"Do you think we got through to Diana?"

Emily shrugged. "I hope so, she was pretty upset. I felt bad for Andy."

He rubbed his hand over Emily's waist and up her side, then down over her ass. "So a funny thing happened before our family meeting. Neil asked me about Candy, what we talked about. You remember when she found out about Michael?"

Emily ran her hand over his chest and looked up at him. He could see her watching him, waiting, listening. "I remember that. You found out she went to see Keith about a divorce. Did you tell Neil?"

"No. She was just weighing her options, you know, and she felt horribly betrayed. She'd never talk to me again if she knew I told Neil."

"You're right. Besides, they seem so much happier."

"Neil said something to me, that you may not always tell me everything."

She stiffened in his arms and went to pull away, then stepped in front of him, putting both her hands on his chest. "Sounds to me as if Neil is trying to stir something up." She glanced over her shoulder to the pool, where Neil was swimming laps.

"So are you keeping things from me?" He didn't like how she was evading his question.

"Yes and no."

"What?" he barked, and she raised an eyebrow at him.

"Seriously, Brad? It's nothing to be worried about. If a problem comes up at home or with the kids, I handle it. There're a lot of everyday things I just handle. I mean, do you tell me every single thing that goes on with the running of the ranch?"

He loved the fire she had in her when she was annoyed.

"Brad, I love you, but don't be an ass. You no more tell me all those little mundane things than I tell you.

Anything major that can't simply be handled, yes, I tell you."

"So you're saying you haven't talked to my brothers or their wives about problems you're having, maybe something between us?" Even to his own ears, he sounded paranoid. The look she leveled on him had him saying, "Never mind. Sounds like Neil trying to rattle my cage."

"Mm-hmm," Emily said as she glanced over her shoulder to Neil again.

There were voices behind him, and he glanced around along with Emily to where Jed walked with Diana. Candy and Laura followed, and Andy was behind them. He noticed how closed off Andy appeared, but he also knew that was Andy's way of dealing with a situation he hadn't quite figured out yet.

They started to the patio table, pulling out chairs and sitting down. He nudged Emily and they followed, pulling out their own chairs. The splashing stopped in the pool, so maybe Neil had noticed all of them sitting poolside.

"What's going on over there?" he called out, his voice echoing in the courtyard.

"Having ourselves a reunion. Come on out and join us," Andy said from where he lounged.

"Anyone bring out any beer?" Neil called out as he swam to the edge and then hopped out of the pool. He reached for a towel on the lounge chair and dried himself off.

"I'll go." Jed slid back his chair, and Diana touched his arm.

"None for me, but I'd love a glass of water."

"You got it," he said, then stopped beside Laura. "Can I get you something, Laura, water, juice, milk?"

"Water is fine for me, too," she said, looking up from where she sat beside Diana.

Brad wondered if he should go help his brother, but then Neil walked over, wearing a white bathrobe tied at the waist, pulling over another chair and putting it in the space between Andy and his wife.

"It's chilly out tonight. Aren't you cold, Neil?" Diana asked as she rubbed her bare arms. She was still in a T-shirt, but she appeared a little more put together than she had been earlier.

"Nah, it's a perfect temperature," Neil said.

"Gabriel looked good, Andy," Brad said. "Is he still in remission?" What Andy and Laura had gone through to save Laura's little boy from leukemia was something that had scared Brad. He couldn't imagine if that were one of his kids.

"He's doing really well. Last checkup, his white blood cell count was still good." Andy clasped his hands in his lap and glanced over at Laura. "He started school this year, and he's been out helping me on the ranch. His riding is getting better. I've had Chelsea and Jeremy riding, too—well, with me."

"He scared me," Laura said. "Had Chelsea sitting in front of him, holding her, when she was just a year old. And then Jeremy. He wants to get them their own pony now. I keep telling him they're too young."

Brad wasn't sure what to say. Jed returned, carrying a tray with beer, stacked glasses, and a jug of water. He put it in the middle of the table, and everyone reached for a beer. Even Candy took the one Neil handed her, and Diana poured a glass of water for herself and Laura.

"That's a great age, Laura," Brad said. "They'll be fine. They couldn't have a better teacher than Andy. He grew up on a horse. We all did." He could feel Emily's eyes on him, knowing they'd had the same argument about their youngest, Becky.

Laura looked to Diana. Maybe she wanted some backup, but Diana just shrugged. "Brad's right, Laura. If there's one thing the Friessen men know, it's horses. And our kids couldn't be in better hands. Andy's not going to let anything happen, you know that."

Laura reluctantly reached over and patted Andy's leg. "Okay."

It was as if he'd won some victory, and he flashed her a cocky smile. "All you needed was Diana's reassurance. Maybe I should have had you call her."

Laura just rolled her eyes.

"I heard you brought in some cattle," Brad said.

"A herd. He got sixty head of longhorns," Laura said. "Noisy things, the way they carry on."

"Longhorns, really?" Neil said.

"Nothing on the level that you and your dad have going on, though. I mean, who has ten thousand acres? But it would be nice to ride out and see all your property. You still have cattle, right?" Andy asked.

"At last count, five hundred head of Angus all at the far west side of the property. It's a long ride out. If you're up to it, we could go tomorrow to the ranch house. There's a foreman and cook who live there all year, and the cowboys hired stay in the camp. Dad has always been the one to handle that, as he said it's in his blood, but with mom down the way she was in rehab, he never made it out once."

"So you've been going out?" Brad asked, because although Neil could ride and handle himself like the rest of them with cattle, livestock, and horses, it wasn't in his blood the way it was Andy's, Jed's, or even his. No, Neil was the only one in the family to have gotten his MBA. He was a business major, not a rancher.

Neil lifted the bottle of beer and swallowed. "Not as often as I should."

Candy had been so quiet, watching everyone, particularly Andy. Brad could see she was bothered by all she'd heard.

"Maybe we could all ride out," Diana said, then looked to Laura. "Except you, of course. No pregnant women on horses."

Both Jed and Andy nearly choked on their beer. "It only took your wife how long to figure that out?" Andy said.

"Hey!" Diana tapped Jed's arm lightly. "I'll have you know that I'm an excellent rider, and I wouldn't have gotten on that horse looking for you—"

"You were ready to give birth, Diana," Andy added.

"Okay, but, Andy, you were there, and it was a good thing, too. And you, Jed, taking that stallion out, getting thrown, and us finding you injured the way you were!"

"Don't forget, Diana, you going into labor." Andy gestured to her with his beer.

Jed was shaking his head, and everyone was laughing.

"Okay, maybe I shouldn't have been on the horse." She raised her hands up in surrender. "The point being, Candy, Emily, what do you say we all ride out with the guys? Would be kind of fun." Diana was sounding so much better, happier, as if a weight had lifted.

"I would like that, but what about the kids?" Emily said.

Diana appeared so sad again, as if all the lightness she'd had a moment ago was gone.

"Ana and Carlos are here. Katy will help, too," Brad said, looking to Emily and then down at Diana. "I think that is a great idea, Diana."

Neil was shaking his head, though, and Candy put her

bottle down on the table before saying, "I'm not sure if Neil is okay with that. He's taken me only once."

"And you know why, Candy," he said to her as if no one else was here.

She rolled her eyes as if they'd argued over this many times and this was one point he wasn't about to budge on. Brad didn't quite understand what the problem was, but evidently it was a sore spot between Neil and Candy. "My husband didn't like the interest the ranch hands showed, although they were just being friendly. Neil didn't like those cowboys being friendly to me."

"You're mine!" he said, looking directly at her. "Any man leering at you the way those dogs were, I won't have it."

"Leering, Neil, seriously?" Diana said, leaning forward.

"Jed, Andy, come on, help me out, here!" Neil looked down at Brad, but he wasn't about to go there with Emily. He had liked it the few times she came out with him on horseback.

"Sorry, Neil, you're on your own," Jed said.

Andy ran his hand over Laura's swollen belly. "And mine is staying back at the estate, where she'll be nice and safe."

Neil looked over at Candy and then down to Brad. "Ah, I'm outnumbered. Well, then, how about after breakfast, we all ride out?"

There was a knock on the bedroom door. Then it opened a crack. "Hello, Becky? It's Candy."

"Come on in, dear." Becky was brushing her hair at her makeup table. She'd already dressed in a blue and green sundress that hung past her knees.

"Rodney asked if I'd come up and check on you."

"You mean he asked you to come in and help me." She could see Candy behind her as she looked in the mirror.

"Yes." She smiled and glanced away, clearing her throat. "He's just—"

"Overworrying, you mean to say," she interjected, as Candy was being too polite.

"Okay." She turned her gaze back to Becky's, and there was lightness and mischief in her eyes. Becky also realized Candy was dressed in blue jeans and a long-sleeved white shirt. Her hair was tied back in a ponytail.

"What are you up to today? I can't remember the last time I've seen you in jeans."

"We're going riding to check on the cattle. We're all going—Neil, Jed, Brad, Andy, Diana, Emily, and me.

Laura is staying here, though, and Ana is going to keep an eye on the kids. Katy is going to help."

"Marvelous! Well, you go and have a good time. I'm so glad Andy is going, too. I didn't think Neil liked you riding out there, though?" No, Becky was sure Neil had made quite a point after the one and only time he'd taken her. He didn't like the way some of the cowboys had stared at his wife. She was gorgeous, and Neil could be a little on the possessive side at times.

"He didn't get much of a choice, considering Diana all but insisted we go." Candy laughed softly. "Besides, I don't think he's going to have to worry too much with all of us going."

Becky put the brush down on the dresser. "I'm glad you're here alone. I wanted to talk to you."

"Oh?" Candy appeared startled.

"It's nothing to worry about, really, but I just wanted to check in with you, see how you're doing. I'm mean, you look so happy." Becky used her cane to turn around in her seat until she was facing her daughter-in-law.

"I am happy," she said, sounding sure of herself. This was a confidence Candy hadn't had even a year ago.

"You were going to leave my son, weren't you?"

Candy was biting her lip. Maybe she didn't want to confide in her. She sat on the padded bench at the foot of the bed and glanced down at her clasped hands. "I don't honestly know, Becky. I guess…I was considering my options. But then you had your stroke, and I couldn't not come."

Becky was watching her, wondering if Candy was still harboring some doubts about her son. "And you love Neil?"

"Oh, love was never the problem. I'll always love Neil, even though, when I found out he had lied to me about

Maria, I felt as if he'd chosen her again. I felt so betrayed, and there was a moment that I hated him. I don't ever want to have that feeling again. He's not the same man he was. He really is trying. I see it in him every day. Where he would have pushed before, he's asking. He really cares what I think, what I feel, so much that he's not just bulldozing ahead, deciding, arranging, and just doing."

Becky had to laugh, because her sons, much like her husband, were very much all alpha.

"Okay, let me rephrase that," Candy said. "He's not nearly as bad, but he still is overprotective."

"And bossy, and he loves you. He's never loved another woman the way he loves you, Candy. I still can't believe he's selling his resort. That was all he talked about for so long," she said.

"I know he loves me, but I also never asked him to sell it." For a minute, Candy seemed defensive.

"I know you didn't. You wouldn't do something like that. I think it's more that my son finally realizes what's really important: you." She pointed at Candy and watched as her daughter-in-law's eyes widened. "You have to know this. You and those beautiful children you have, Cat and Michael, he'd do anything for you, but he'll still always be Neil—my brilliant, independent son who always has some huge idea for a project."

Candy actually laughed. "He says he'll be happy at our little acreage by Brad and Emily, that he'll figure out what he's going to do after we get back. But you're right. I see the wheels spinning. I'm almost afraid to know what he'll come up with."

"But you're all in?" Becky asked. She had to know.

"I'm all in." Candy smiled. "And we're getting there. It's not back where we were, but it's a stronger place after all we've been through. I don't want back what we had. I wasn't happy. I was smothered, and I felt my voice disappearing."

"But you don't now?" Becky said. Candy had such a confidence now, no longer the same scared young woman she'd first met running out of the house, chasing down the baby donkey who was in her flower garden. "You almost remind me of me."

Candy appeared confused.

"I didn't have a lot of confidence when I married Rodney. I had to find my feet, and you've done that, but you didn't make the mistakes I did, Candy. You stayed true to yourself."

She nodded. "You know, when Rodney told me your story while he sat at your bedside, I realized every one of us has something. It was your story of how bad it had gotten that made all the difference for me, Becky, and I realized that if I wanted my marriage, my family, then I, too, was going to have to do something about it."

"I'm so glad, Candy. It was very hard for me to listen to Rodney tell you about my indiscretion. Even though I thought he had cheated on me—and, in a way, he was paying attention to another woman—for me to fall for Todd Friessen's charms…" She shook her head, remembering back to how sympathetic he had been, visiting his brother, listening to his pretty young sister-in-law vent about Rodney and her marriage dissolving around them. The first time he kissed her, he'd said all the right things about how much he appreciated her. Looking back now, she saw what a fool she'd been. She shut her eyes, trying to block out the memory, and felt Candy's hand on her arm.

"Are you all right?"

"Yeah, the problem is when you've done something so awful in your past, you always carry the memory of it with you. It never goes away."

"You should tell Neil."

She shook her head. "No, Candy. You needed to hear it, but no one else does." She grabbed her cane and stood up. "Let's go downstairs, and then you kids head off and have some fun."

CHAPTER

Twenty~One

Being back in the saddle was something Neil had always enjoyed, not to the extent that Jed and Andy did, and even Brad was more of a country boy than he'd ever be, but he'd climbed in the saddle less and less lately.

It was almost a two-hour ride to the perimeter of where the ranch house was located and the five hundred cattle grazed in a fenced-off area behind it. They could have driven around and gotten there much sooner, but there was something about riding across the range, here, sandy in parts, grassy in some, and now bare, dry land with the blazing hot sun above.

He glanced over to Jed, Brad, and Andy, who were wearing cowboy hats they'd borrowed from his dad, riding just ahead. The three of them had been determined to lead. Candy, Diana, and Emily followed behind, chatting away. Diana and Emily wore ball caps, and Candy was wearing the Stetson he'd bought her a year ago. It was white and such a contrast to her dark hair. She sat so tall on Sable, her gelding. They had a connection few ever had with horses, and he was proud to be riding with her.

"Hey, you! I have a bone to pick with you," Emily said and trotted over to him. She was wearing a short-sleeved shirt, and even though Brad had nagged her to put on sunscreen, Neil could see she was going to have a nice burn by the time they got back.

She was bouncing a bit in the saddle of the Arabian she was riding. Emily was not as skilled a rider as Candy, and even Diana was much more comfortable on a horse, but then, she spent a lot of time riding with Jed.

"That sounds serious. You should put on your jacket, cover your arms."

She frowned. "Neil, are you kidding? It's like ninety degrees out here."

"Em, you're going to be paying for it if you don't."

She held the reins in her right hand, walking beside him on the horse he was riding, Jessop, his father's gray Arabian. He was spooky at times, but Neil could handle him.

"Neil, why did you tell my husband that I keep things from him?" She was annoyed with him. He'd never seen Emily look like this, not with him. With Brad, yes, as a mother, maybe, but not to this degree.

"Don't you?" he asked.

She appeared shocked as her eyes widened. "No!" she said and glanced to where her husband was riding next to Andy.

"So you tell him every single thing you're thinking, doing, everything that has come up that you've had to fix or handle to make everything run smoothly? Or is it that you censor and tell him only what he needs to know, because you, as his wife, are trying to make things easier? I'm pretty sure if you told him everything, he'd spend more time listening to you recount a day of boring than having some much-needed fun."

He wasn't sure if she'd kicked her horse or what, as her mount took off a little too fast and Emily almost lost her seat. Neil reached over and grabbed the reins, pulling her over and slowing him to a walk.

"Thank you," she said, a little breathless.

"If you get upset, your horse is going to pick it up. And squeezing your horse's side with your legs, he's going to think you want him to go faster." Neil let go of the reins, and Emily walked her horse beside him again.

"Neil, you're twisting everything. Of course I don't tell Brad all the mundane details, just like he doesn't tell me all the mundane details of how many bales of hay he fed the cattle. What you insinuated to Brad had my husband thinking I'm keeping some pretty big secrets from him. I'm not, I wouldn't do that. I may have my own thoughts about things, same as you, but do you share every single thing you're thinking?"

He really had stirred up something, all because Brad was speaking with his wife, and Candy had confided in him and he still didn't know what they'd talked about. He knew he should let it go, but it was hard when you loved someone so much and had almost destroyed everything between both of you. He was worried about what they'd discussed.

"Hey, what's going on back there?" Brad trotted over to Emily, glancing from her to Neil. Jed, Andy, Candy, and Diana also closed in.

"I almost lost control of the horse. Neil grabbed the reins, but I'm fine. I'm not the expert horsemen you all are."

"Just do what I told you, Em," Brad said. "Keep your reins loose, your hand forward, and remember your seat."

Emily rolled her eyes at the way her husband was hovering.

"Your wife was admonishing me for stirring things up between you," Neil said.

Everyone looked at Neil with surprise. Candy slid down the shades she was wearing, and he could tell she was wondering what he'd said or done.

"Let's just tell everyone, Neil," Emily said. "Neil led my husband to believe that I may be keeping things from him, which I'm not. What I mean by that is the important things, not the everyday boring details."

Even Andy circled his horse beside Neil. "What's going on?" he said in a low voice, as if Neil had lost his mind.

What had he started? All because of his own insecurities. He looked to Candy, who was still watching him, riding side by side with Diana. "I was upset because, Candy, you told me you had Brad to confide in." He stopped talking then, because as he started thinking about what he just said, he realized he was doing everything he promised Candy he wouldn't.

"I don't understand, Neil. How did that have anything to do with you telling Brad Emily's keeping things from him?" Candy asked. Diana was giving him a confused look.

Right at this moment, he would give anything for the ground to open up or a herd of cattle to come racing their way, just enough to distract them. "Because I'm an idiot, okay? I talked to Brad, and he told me he had talked with you, and he felt that he had every right." He could feel everyone staring at him, some a little more heatedly than others.

"Let's back up here a second, Neil. Did you or did you not say you were going to speak to Diana because she needed someone other than her husband to speak to, and did Jed come asking you what you spoke with his wife about, or saying that he was upset you spoke with her?" Candy said.

"You spoke with my wife?" Jed asked, also circling in front of them. He didn't sound happy.

"Jed, what we talked about wasn't anything I was keeping from you. It was just another perspective on this same old crap with my mother—and for Neil to point out that I need to start dressing better and stop hiding my beauty," Diana said as she glanced Neil's way.

Candy actually laughed. And Jed…well, Neil was sure he was about to snarl by the face he made.

"Okay, the point being, I didn't ask Brad to tell me what you said, Candy. Did I, Brad?" He could feel his big brother just watching him, and for a moment he wondered whether Brad was going to say anything.

"No, he didn't, Candy, but I also told you, Neil, that I wouldn't tell you, because Candy is family, and at the time she was very alone. Candy, you know you can talk to me anytime," Brad said, and Candy actually had confidence in her smile as she nodded.

"Thank you, Brad," she said, then looked over at Neil and urged her horse over, coming up between him and Emily. Andy had been riding silently beside him, taking them both in. "Neil, do you need me to tell you what I talked to Brad about?" Candy asked, and he wanted to say yes. He was dying to say yes.

"Maybe one day, when you want me to know," he said to her, and she nodded, her smile deepening. "Hey, but there was one other thing you said before, and I have to ask. You said it helped, talking to Brad, but it was my father and mother that convinced you. When was this, and what did they do to convince you?"

He wasn't sure what it was, but her smile faded. She

glanced over at Andy, who was staring back at her, and then she took a breath, gazing forward. "It was after your mom's stroke. Your dad knew how bad it was between us, and when your mom woke, he shared something that helped me decide how important it was to try."

Neil glanced over at Andy, who was frowning. Maybe he was as confused as Neil was. Maybe everyone else was wondering the same thing, by the confused looks on their faces.

"Dad shared some advice?" Brad asked Candy.

Candy was shaking her head. She opened her mouth to say something, and Neil could tell that whatever it was, she was feeling mighty awkward. "Sometimes, you know when someone shares something with you that makes all the difference? Well, it's something personal, and it's not mine to share." She looked straight ahead, and everyone stared at her, because whatever this was had to be pretty big.

Neil glanced over at Andy, and he shrugged. When he glanced back at his wife, the expression on her face as she looked at Andy was far from happy. Neil wasn't sure what else he could say to Candy to help her feel better about his cousin.

"Hey, hold up!" Jed called from up ahead where he topped the ridge. When they all climbed the sandy dune where the grassland started and looked down to the small ranch house, to the field where the cattle should have been grazing, all they could see was an empty field, a barn door swaying in the wind, and not a soul around.

At the sound of the gunshot, Neil didn't think. He just grabbed Candy from her horse and hit the ground.

Twenty~Two

"Is everyone okay?" Brad shouted as he grabbed Emily and pulled her against him on the ground. As soon as he heard the shot, his blood had run cold. He was now on the ground with Emily, covering her head. "Keep your head down!" he shouted at her. The horse had bolted the other way, back from where they'd come, and he glanced to his right to see Neil also on the ground.

"Brad, you're heavy. I can't breathe," Emily cried out, loud enough he could hear, but it was muffled, too.

He scooted back down the hill in the sand and grass, dragging Emily with him. "Keep your head down!" he shouted again at her, keeping his arm around her waist. He was on one knee, and looked over at Neil, who was about twenty feet away. Candy was beside him, scooting down the hill.

"Brad, did you see who was shooting?" Neil called out and glanced behind him. Brad was sweating through his long-sleeved shirt, feeling the sand in his mouth and grit on his tongue.

"No, I didn't see anyone."

"Brad, what's going on?" Emily sounded really scared. Hell, he was scared! He didn't like the fact that not one of them had thought to carry a rifle. His dad had how many guns locked in the gun cabinet in the shed? Even at home, he'd have slid one in behind his saddle, mainly for cougars.

"I don't know, Em. Just stay down, stay under me."

She was squirming as he put his hand on the back of her head. She reached back, and there was blood on her fingers.

"You're bleeding," he said, and he grabbed her hand as she tried to look.

"What? I can't be. Must've cut my hand when you tackled me."

Seeing the blood—even though it wasn't bad, really, just a little cut—made him worry about what could have happened to Emily. It was a place he didn't want to go. "Are you hurt anywhere else? Neil, how are you and Candy?" Brad called out.

"No, I'm okay, Brad. I can't even feel anything," Emily said.

"It's the adrenaline racing," Neil said. "Candy, are you hurt?" He was running his hands over her and looking behind him. "Jed, Diana?"

Jed was at the bottom of the hill, holding his horse's reins in one hand, squatting down, with Diana behind him. "We're okay!" he shouted. "Andy went after the horses."

Brad could see the dust trail and, in the distance, Andy racing after the horses.

"What the hell's going on here, Neil?" Jed didn't sound happy.

"I don't know. I haven't been here in weeks. This was Dad's thing. He came out here almost every day but stopped completely after Mom's stroke. We've just let our foreman, Pedro, run things."

"Maybe that wasn't such a good thing. Didn't see any cattle, either. What do you think, rustlers?"

"I don't know, Brad. I'm not the cowboy, remember?" Neil snapped, and Brad felt someone shake his foot. He jerked his head to see Jed crouched down behind him. Diana was still crouched at the bottom of the hill, holding the horse.

"Get Em and Candy down the hill with Diana. We need to get them out of here," Jed said.

"Jed, we're kind of sitting ducks. I hope Andy decided to go for help."

Neil reached in his pocket and dragged out his cell phone. He pressed some numbers and held the phone to his ear. "Pedro, where the hell are you?"

Brad was watching his brother look up, and then he stood up, the stupid idiot. "Neil, get down!"

Neil waved at Brad. "That was us coming, so where the hell is the herd?" He slid the phone away from his month and looked over the hill. "That was Pedro shooting. Come on, Pedro. Walk out on the front porch. Show me the gun," he said back in the phone.

"Neil!" Candy pulled at him. "Get down."

"It's fine." Then he was waving at someone. He turned to Brad. "That was Pedro shooting. He thought we were the cowboys who stole the herd coming back."

Brad rolled over on his back, and Emily scooted up as Jed jogged back to Diana. He stood up, still keeping his hand on Emily's shoulder just to make sure she stayed down until he was sure it was okay.

He saw a plump Mexican wearing an apron waving from the porch. Then the man started down the steps, looking right and then left, kicking up dust as he walked toward them, rifle still in his hand.

"Whatcha doing? You didn't think to call first? I could have shot your head off!" Pedro called out and stopped halfway, gesturing wildly.

Neil brushed himself off and reached for Candy, helping her up. He gave Brad a frazzled look and started down the hill toward Pedro.

"What the hell happened here? Why didn't you let us know rustlers showed up?"

"They tied me up. I just broke free. Heard you and thought you were them."

Neil was almost to Pedro when Jed appeared beside him. Emily had sand in her hair and was covered in grit. He could tell she wasn't happy.

"So rustlers, seriously?" she said.

"Apparently." Brad looked around, wondering if they were still nearby. "Come on, I don't feel like standing out here in the middle of nowhere and being a target." He tugged on Emily, and Jed mounted his horse, pulling Diana up behind him and then starting off at a trot, leaving Brad walking with his wife.

"Not the easy ride you expected." He slid his arm around her.

She gazed up at him, a piece of grass sticking out in her hair, her hat long gone. "Well, seems to be the story of our life, Brad." She squeezed his hip with her hand.

"I guess you're right. I never thought of it that way."

She bumped her hip into him playfully. "Not that I'm complaining, but whatever would we do with a nice, easy ride?"

He loved to see her smile. "We'd probably be bored to tears."

Twenty~Three

The garden had been transformed into a paradise, which had surprisingly been all Rodney. He'd arranged all the details with Ana, more flowers, chairs for the family before an archway that was laced with white lilies. It was breathtaking. Even an open tent had been set up for the food and two large tables, with one for the kids. The tablecloths were white, the crystal was out, and the table was set with Becky's good china and silverware.

Today, she had so much to be thankful for: her family, her sons, their wives, even Andy. She still couldn't believe the sight yesterday late afternoon when Diana, Emily, Candy, and her sons all rode in. Carlos had helped her sons and Andy with the horses, brushing them down and taking them back to the stables behind the cottage that Carlos lived in with Ana. But it was the dirt and grit, the disheveled appearance of her daughter-in-laws as their kids raced toward them, that had Becky giving them a second look from the lounger she sat in beside the pool. Laura, who was such a sweet girl, so much younger than Andy, was rubbing her swollen belly and sitting next to Becky in a second lounger under the shaded umbrella.

Diana, holding Christopher, and Danny beside her, sat at the foot of Laura's lounger. "You should be glad you didn't come," she said.

"You three look a lot worse for wear. What did you do, roll in the dirt?" Becky asked.

Candy pulled over a chair as Cat came running over and hugged her. She pulled her up on her lap and held her. "In a manner of speaking, we did—when Neil tackled me off my horse."

"Brad was so heavy and ground my face into the sand. I can still taste it on my tongue." Emily was walking slow and awkward, her hair falling out of her ponytail and appearing tangled on the side. She tapped Diana's shoulder as she walked past and grabbed another padded chair, dragging it over beside Candy. Little Becky raced over then and hugged her mom, dripping from the pool. "Oh, Becky, you're getting me all wet."

"Why are you so dirty, Mom?"

Grandma Becky wanted to know the same thing.

"Well, you see, we were riding across the range, and as soon as we topped the hill—"

"There was a gunshot!" Diana jumped in, glancing over at Emily. The kids' eyes all widened.

"The next thing I knew, I was on the ground—"

"And Brad was yelling at me to stay down," Emily said, interrupting Candy.

"I fell off my horse, and Jed grabbed my shirt collar and was dragging me behind him." Diana brushed back her short bangs. "I didn't have a chance to see what was going on, because Jed wouldn't let me. He was still holding his horse."

"Ours were gone, racing the other way." Candy was shaking her head. "But Andy went after them."

"I was impressed he came back with all of them," Diana said.

Becky didn't know what to think, considering her daughter-in-laws were so calm. Laura was watching them, wide eyed. Becky wondered what expression was on her own face. "So no one was hurt?"

The three women looked at each other. "No," Candy said.

"But there was a gunshot? Who was shooting?" Becky asked when she saw Rodney come out of the house, holding the phone.

"I just heard," he said to Diana, Emily, and Candy. "Are you all right?"

"Would someone please tell me what's going on? Rodney?" Becky said, moving forward, putting her legs over the edge of the lounger.

"Pedro fired off a shot, thought they were cattle rustlers."

"What?" both Becky and Laura said at the same time.

Laura was looking a little upset. "Where's Andy? Is he all right?"

Diana patted Laura's leg. "He's fine, but leave it to Andy to not only find our horses but spot the herd of cattle grazing. I don't know how he did it, but we were sitting there at the ranch house with Pedro," Diana said.

"What a mess that was! Chairs knocked over, breakfast still on the table, half eaten," Emily started.

"You didn't have to clean up, Emily," Diana said, and Candy smiled.

"Well, I didn't know what else to do or how long we'd be stuck there. The flies were buzzing everywhere." Emily had little Becky on her knee, wide eyed, listening, her head turning, trying to listen as they told the story.

"What about the rustlers?" Grandma Becky wanted to get up and shake her daughter-in-laws, who appeared far too calm.

"Oh, they were long gone, or not around," Diana said. "But here we are, Jed, Neil, and Brad interrogating Pedro, who apparently had been tied up and had just gotten himself loose, about what happened, when we hear this god-awful noise of cows coming."

"And we look out, and over the hill come all these cows," Emily said.

"Black and red cows," Diana said. "And they just keep coming and coming. There are hundreds."

"Angus," Candy said as she leaned on her hand. Becky had never seen her so amused.

"Right, Angus, not that I know the breeds," Diana said. "And then Jed and Neil, Brad, and Pedro are suddenly running to the open gate that leads out to the field."

"The herd knew where home was, and they just wandered back into their field, and there was Andy, bringing up the herd with our horses. He's holding the reins in both hands, moving back and forth, and he has no idea that there were cattle rustlers because he's missed the entire conversation with Pedro. The only reason he knew the cattle belonged to Neil and Rodney was the Friessen brand," Candy added. "And you should have seen Brad and Neil take a strip off Andy! Never seen them so mad."

"I think they were more scared that he could've been shot if he'd stumbled across the rustlers. There were four of them. Two were cowboys who worked for you," Diana said. "Jed still hasn't said a word to Andy. He's pretty upset with him."

"Damn foolish thing to do, but I'm glad you're all okay," Rodney said. "I'm going to have a word with my sons and Andy."

"That was the most fun I've had in a long time," Diana said and giggled. She exchanged a glance with Candy and Emily before they all started laughing.

Even dinner had been lively as they all recounted the story, and the tale got better as the night went on. But it was later, after a few beers, that Becky spotted Andy and Jed outside alone. Whatever they were saying had Jed reaching his arm out and hugging Andy.

Having her entire family here meant everything to Becky. As she walked up the red carpet to the archway, she thought everyone looked amazing. Her sons were dashing in their suits and ties, Candy in a purple strapless gown, Diana in a lovely pink backless dress, and Emily in a simple red dress with spaghetti straps and a fitted bodice. Her daughter-in-laws were absolutely stunning.

"Aunt Becky, you look so good," Andy said. Her charming nephew knew how to dress the part in his dark suit and red tie. He had a cut above his eye, apparently the only mishap from the previous day's adventure.

"How's your head?" she asked him.

"It's fine," he said as she reached up and touched beside the small cut. "Okay, already! Laura has been fussing over me since she saw it."

"Well, let me tell you that was a pretty foolish thing to do," she said again even though she'd said it a few times already the night before.

"How many times do I have to tell everyone I didn't know there were rustlers? I didn't see any, just the herd, and there was no one around. It's possible they were planning on coming back."

"It's good for all of us they didn't," Becky said.

"Well, they won't like the reception they get if they do," Andy said just as Laura approached in a white and blue maternity dress that was so flattering Becky couldn't help wondering if Andy was still buying her clothes.

"No, your uncle Rodney took care of that. He has enough cowhands and security over there that no one would be foolish enough to show up." She patted Andy's shoulder when Laura slid her hand on his arm. "You two, I'm so glad you came. You're family, Andy and Laura. Your uncle Rodney and I wanted all of you here."

Andy leaned down and kissed her cheek, then escorted his wife over to some chairs on the other side of the yard. The kids were running everywhere, dressed in their finest.

Rodney slid his hand over the shoulder of her ivory gown. It had a fitted bodice with short sleeves and stopped just past her knees. "Are you ready?" he said.

"I am. No minister?" she asked, wondering if there was another surprise yet.

He just shook his head. "I married you once before a minister. For forty years, it's been only you and me who've shared our vows, and every anniversary, those vows you said to me and I said to you have meant more to me in my heart than on the day we were married."

How could it be possible to love the man she fell in love with forty-five years ago even more today? "And having our children here?" she asked, but she already knew the answer as he gazed over her head at the family they had created together.

"Makes this day even better."

Twenty~Four

E veryone was laughing and talking. Wine was flowing, the food was spectacular, and Andy couldn't remember ever being happier. For the first time, after always being on the outside looking in, he felt as if he was now a part of a family. Oh, he was a Friessen, but he was Todd Friessen's son, not his uncle Rodney's, a man he looked up to with admiration.

The love that flowed between his aunt Becky and uncle Rodney had left him a little misty eyed when he'd listened to them declare their love for each other. They were such an inspiration. The ceremony had been a simple one, with only the family to witness this private special moment.

"You've been awfully quiet tonight," Candy said, joining him where he stood at the back of the tent. She had been so distant since his arrival. He'd often wondered what she really thought of him. He wasn't a fool and hadn't missed the uncertainty in her expression, the frowns she cast his way when she thought he wasn't looking.

"It was a great dinner, a nice ceremony." He glanced down at her. "You look very nice tonight," he added. The way her gown hung off her breasts and molded to her curves, he'd have to have been blind not to notice what a spectacular woman she was.

"Thank you, Andy. Everyone looks great tonight. The kids had fun. Looks like you have your hands full with Chelsea and Jeremy! I don't think they've stopped running with Christopher and Danny all night."

Of course he smiled. He couldn't help smiling—he loved his children. Chelsea looked more and more like Laura every day, and Jeremy had his dark looks. With Gabriel, he could still see, at times, the young man who'd fathered him, but Gabriel was now his legally, and with another child on the way, he considered himself fortunate. He really did look up to his uncle.

"You and Neil seem happy," he said. They did, and he was relieved that his cousin had held on to his wife, his family.

"We are. We had a lot to work through, still do. But there's hope."

He wondered if she had any idea what Neil would do for her. "You have a husband who loves you and would move mountains for you. But look at his role models. My aunt and uncle are devoted to each other. I wonder if Brad, Neil, and Jed know how lucky they are, having two parents who love them and are committed to each other and their family—parents who have never strayed." Andy swallowed a mouthful of bourbon from the glass he was holding.

Candy was staring straight ahead with an odd look on her face. But then, what did she have for family? Maybe she, too, was struggling with this. "Do you ever talk to your father?"

Now why would she ask that? "Todd?" He shook his head. "Not since I married Laura and squashed his and my mother's big political plans. No, it's best if Todd Friessen stays out of my life." His mother, too, even though it had hurt him more than he could admit to anyone not to have parents who loved him like Rodney and Becky loved his cousins. He had left a place that had always been his, moving to Montana with Laura, just the two of them, with no family around.

"Just in case I didn't say it, Andy, thanks for going after our horses and coming back for us." She reached up and patted the side of his shoulder, then glanced over to where Neil was holding a sleeping Michael.

"Hey, don't thank me, Candy. We're family. Family always has each other's backs."

She gave him a slow, easy smile and then touched his arm again. "You're right, Andy. We do," she said, and she walked away with her head high toward her husband, taking the sleeping baby from him. Andy couldn't help being happy for his cousin, seeing Neil and Candy figure out what was important, to have a family and a love that was strong.

But then, Neil had parents who'd married for love, stayed together in love, and made it work. He envied that. Even though Rodney and Becky weren't his parents, they were still family, his aunt and uncle. At times, though, it made him ache, wondering how his father could be so different from his own brother. Maybe one day, his father would figure out how wrong he'd been. He could only hope.

"Hey, Andy, get over here!" Brad called out to him, waving from where he sat with his wife on his lap.

"Coming," Andy said as he walked over to the family —his family.

Turn the page for a sneak peek of
*THE BLOODLINE, 'A 2016 Readers' Favorite Award Winner in
Romance' and the next book in* THE FRIESSENS
Available in print, audio & eBook.

Andy Friessen has two guarantees in life:

1. His wife, Laura, and his children are safe
   from the control of his family.

2. A safety deposit box holds evidence that
   could blow his mother's world apart.

But nothing is ever simple or easy, and one night tragedy strikes, yanking the rug from under him. This time, secrets and lies could destroy the solid foundation he's built for his family.

Chapter 1

The numbers just weren't adding up. As Andy stared at the spreadsheet on his iMac, his eyes started to go blurry. He could just pass this off to his accountant, but he felt it was important to know every detail of his business before he contracted any work out. Right now, he was missing five more longhorns from the extensive herd he had amassed.

"Andy, do you want some tea?"

He didn't need to glance up to his wife, Laura, to know she was already bringing him some, the herbal kind he couldn't believe he actually liked. He leaned back in the dark leather chair behind his desk, neat and dust free, just the way he liked it.

"How did you know?" He took the steaming mug, breathing in the orange spice and taking a welcome sip.

Laura leaned down on the desk, resting her arms and just looking at him. She had such a soft smile, so genuine that she made him feel he could do anything. "Oh, you've been working in here for hours, holed up. Heard you swear a few times, so I knew things weren't quite working out the way you wanted." She had their baby monitor hooked to the waistband of her jeans—jeans she filled out in a way that drew every man's eye. Some women had great asses, and his wife was one of them.

She was a welcome distraction, considering there had seemed to be a constant loss of cattle over the past twelve weeks. "It'll be fine," he said. "The baby asleep?" He took another welcome sip as the warmth eased some of his frustration. So did she, the way she leaned on his desk, giving him an eyeful of her cleavage. Andy needed the distraction. He was getting worked up because someone or something was taking his cattle from him—taking what was his, what belonged to his family. Right now, someone was messing with his livelihood, and his next move would be to hire more help to find out what was happening to his sizeable herd: three hundred head of longhorns, including breeding stock and yearlings. It was the yearlings who were getting picked off.

"She went down about an hour ago," Laura said. "Sarah's so good, just like Chelsea. She's an angel, the way she sleeps on her side, her tiny little thumb in her mouth."

He didn't think he'd ever get tired of hearing everything about his children. Sarah, the baby, had been born eight weeks ago. It had been an easy birth. They'd made it to the hospital just in time, and Laura had eased through her contractions. Two hours later, Sarah had been born—an easy baby, a content baby, and the youngest of their four.

"What about the munchkins? No one's been bugging me," Andy said, not that he'd ever once considered his twins, Chelsea and Jeremy, who were just a few months shy of three, an annoyance. They were happy, healthy, full of life, radiating joy from their innocent smiles, which filled his heart so full at times he thought it would burst.

"Napping, too. Jeremy insisted he wasn't tired and argued with me up until he fell asleep, and that was before I even got Chelsea tucked in."

He reached out and skimmed his thumb over Laura's cheekbone, under her eyes. The dark circles she'd had from nursing the baby the first few weeks had disappeared, and she now had a healthy glow. Her blond hair had a natural wave it hadn't before, and it was pinned up in a messy bun that made her look gorgeous. Did she have any idea what she did to him? He doubted it. "So there's just you and me and a quiet house for…" He reached out, sliding his hand down Laura's side as she leaned on the desk beside him.

"What are you doing?" she teased as he put his tea down, and she straddled his lap, her arms linked around his neck.

He couldn't get over how well she fit him, how she moved against him, a touch, a breath. Giving herself to him was a gift he had once taken for granted. What a fool he'd been. Never again would he disrespect Laura or be ungrateful for all she had given him: his children, her love, herself. "Touching my wife," he said. Maybe it was arrogant and selfish, but he could only hold himself back from loving Laura for so long. He'd been patient for months during her late pregnancy and after, and he was making up for lost time, needing to bury himself in her heat, in her love, and connect with her.

He ran his large hand down her stomach, which still had a slight bulge from where she'd carried his children. It was a miracle how his seed had created the lives that filled this house, making it a home. His family.

Her breath hissed, and he could feel the way she trembled as he ran his hand up and over both her generous breasts, which fed his baby girl. His other hand followed as he shoved his fingers in her hair, pulling it loose, pulling her down so he could taste those full, kissable red lips.

Her eyes…the green had become brighter, he swore, over the past year. For a woman so young, she had carried a lifetime of living, of hurt, of love. It was in her expression, the shadow of her eyes, always there, and those memories were the first place she went whenever something bad happened. Then she'd stop and take a breath. He saw it time and again, thankful it was happening less as the days passed and she was starting to believe that Andy would always protect her and keep everything bad from touching her and the children. If something happened, he wanted her first thought to be free of worry, knowing she was safe, believing he'd protect her and their family.

She leaned in to his touch, and she didn't have to say a word for him to know she trusted him, giving herself to him so freely to touch, to caress, to taste, and to be with whenever he needed her. She was so damn responsive to him, and he didn't think he'd ever have enough of his woman.

He kissed her neck as his hands slid under her light T-shirt, lifting it over her head and tossing it to the floor. His other hand slid up her back, over the soft skin and up her spine, and again she pressed closer to him, her hands gripping his shoulders tighter. She gasped as he unclasped her bra and divested her of it, and he stood up and laid her on her back against the glass top of his desk. She was so bewitching as he pulled away and slid her zipper down, pulling off her jeans and socks until she was naked on his desk, and then he just studied her for a second, every inch of her creamy white skin: the tiny marks across her almost flat stomach, her breasts, which had always been a generous handful but had grown a cup during her pregnancy. They were firm and large, and he savored the moments he could run his tongue over her nipples and kiss and touch every inch of her after he made love to her over and over, marking her so she knew she belonged to him. He could be gentle and rough, hurried and slow, but every time he came in her it was with her coming around him. It was a connection so strong, so powerful, and one he had never expected.

"Are you going to just stare at me, or are you going to have your way with me before the kids wake?" She raised her arms above her head and spread her legs so he could see all of her.

He said nothing as he unzipped his jeans, freeing his erection. Laura wiggled on the desk as her face flushed, maybe anticipating how he'd take her.

As he ran his hand up her thigh and then spread her wider, he took her deep and hard, forcing another squeak from her lips as he moved the way he knew she loved. Being together was instinctual as she wrapped her legs around his waist and ran her hands up his chest, clutching his shoulders and hanging on while Andy made love to her, drawing out just enough that he could send her over the edge and have her scream out his name as he filled her over and over.

About the Author

Follow Lorhainne on Bookbub to receive alerts on New Releases and Sales and join her mailing list at Lorhainne-Eckhart.com for her Monday Blog, all book news, give-aways and FREE reads. With over 120 books, audiobooks, and multiple series published and available at all, retailers now translated into six languages. She is a multiple recipient of the Readers' Favorite Award for Suspense and Romance, and lives in the Pacific Northwest on an island, is the mother of three, her oldest has autism and she is an advocate for never giving up on your dreams.

"Lorhainne Eckhart has this uncanny way of just hitting the spot every time with her books."

(CAROLINE L., REVIEWER)

The O'Connells: *The O'Connells of Livingston, Montana are not your typical family. A riveting collection of stories surrounding the ups and downs of what goes on within a family but also with some suspense, angst and of course a bit of romance thrown in for good measure. "I thought I loved the Friessens, but I absolutely adore the O'Connell's. Each and every book has different genres of stories, but the one thing in common is how she is able to wrap it around the family, which is the heart of each story." (C. Logue)*

The Friessens: *An emotional big family romance series, the Friessen family siblings find their relationships tested, lay their hearts on the line, and discover lasting love! "Lorhainne Eckhart is one of my go to authors when I want* *a guaranteed good book. So many twists and turns, but also so much love and such a strong sense of family." (Lora W., Reviewer)*

The Parker Sisters: *The Parker Sisters are a close-knit family, and like any other family they have their ups and downs. Eckhart has crafted another intense family drama… "The character development is outstanding, and the emotional investment is high…" (Aherman, Reviewer)*

The McCabe Brothers: *Join the five McCabe siblings on their journeys to the dark and dangerous side of love! An intense, exhilarating collection of romantic thrillers you won't want to miss. — "Eckhart has a new series that is definitely worth the read. The queen of the family saga started this series with a spin-off of her wildly successful Friessen series." From a Readers' Favorite award—winning author and "queen of the family saga" (Aherman)*

Billy Jo McCabe Mystery: *The social worker and the cop, an unlikely couple drawn together on a small, secluded Pacific Northwest island where nothing is as it seems. Protecting the innocent comes at a cost, and what seems to be a sleepy, quiet town is anything but.*

Lorhainne loves to hear from her readers! You can connect with me at:
www.LorhainneEckhart.com
lorhainneeckhart.le@gmail.com

In the Charm
Unexpected Consequences
It Was Always You
The First Time I Saw You
Welcome to My Arms
Welcome to Boston
I'll Always Love You
Ground Rules
A Reason to Breathe
You Are My Everything
Anything For You
The Homecoming
Stay Away From My Daughter
The Bad Boy
A Place of Our Own
The Visitor
All About Devon
Long Past Dawn
How to Heal a Heart
Keep Me In Your Heart

The O'Connells
The Neighbor
The Third Call
The Secret Husband
The Quiet Day
The Commitment
The Missing Father
The Hometown Hero
Justice
The Family Secret
The Fallen O'Connell
The Return of the O'Connells
And The She Was Gone

The Stalker
The O'Connell Family Christmas
The Girl Next Door
Broken Promises
The Gatekeeper
The Hunted

The McCabe Brothers
Don't Stop Me (Vic)
Don't Catch Me (Chase)
Don't Run From Me (Aaron)
Don't Hide From Me (Luc)
Don't Leave Me (Claudia)
Out of Time

A Billy Jo McCabe Mystery
Nothing As it Seems
Hiding in Plain Sight
The Cold Case
The Trap
Above the Law
The Stranger at the Door
The Children
The Last Stand
The Charity
The Sacrifice

The Street Fighter
Finding Home
Finding Honor

The Wilde Brothers
The One (Joe and Margaret)
The Honeymoon, A Wilde Brothers Short

Friendly Fire (Logan and Julia)
Not Quite Married, A Wilde Brothers Short
A Matter of Trust (Ben and Carrie)
The Reckoning, A Wilde Brothers Christmas
Traded (Jake)
Unforgiven (Samuel)
The Holiday Bride

Married in Montana
His Promise
Love's Promise
A Promise of Forever

The Parker Sisters
Thrill of the Chase
The Dating Game
Play Hard to Get
What We Can't Have
Go Your Own Way
A June Wedding

Kate & Walker
One Night
Edge of Night
Last Night

Walk the Right Road Series
The Choice
Lost and Found
Merkaba
Bounty
Blown Away: The Final Chapter
He Came Back

Advance Praise for
Orion O'Brien and the Phantoms of Wakarusa

"Orion and Ollie O'Brien and their friends, Sal and Sofi Martelli, expect a boring week-long visit to their aunt's and uncle's blueberry farm near Baldwin, Kansas, but are surprised to find the freedom of farm life and the fear and excitement of discovering two phantoms from the Civil War era. Once again, history is seamlessly woven into the storyline. Without even realizing it, young readers will learn factual details about the history of Baker University and the importance of the Civil War Battle of Black Jack."

SHANNON SHORE HOWELL
Direct descendant of Samuel T. Shore, Co-Captain with John Brown at the Black Jack Battle

"This book is just plain inspiring and fun to read. There are many positive things you could say about it. In some ways, it is definitely sad. But some parts are really fun and happy. I personally like the Phantoms, because they have such a never-ending, relentless back story. I would recommend this book to any person seven years old or older. Please write more books like this, Fran Borin."

BRANDON EDDINGS
Age 10, McLouth, KS

"Orion O'Brien and the Phantoms of Wakarusa is a very good book because you learn about the Underground Railroad. It is also a great ghost story with an amazing plot twist."

GIBSON DONNELLY
Age 10, Prairie Village, KS

"Orion O'Brien and the Phantoms of Wakarusa is the third in a series of finely crafted historical fiction books about eleven-year-old Orion O'Brien and her younger brother, Ollie. In this volume, the two again encounter phantoms–this time, the ghosts of two siblings who tragically died in 1863. Middle-grade students and others will enjoy following their dramatic adventures as they attempt to solve a mystery involving freedom seekers on the Kansas Underground Railroad. This book helps fill a gap in the literature about an often-overlooked period in our nation's history–the pre-Civil War period."

JUDITH SWEETS
Historian and author specializing in Territorial Kansas, Underground Railroad and Douglas County topics

"I really like that this book talks about Kansas history and the burning of Lawrence, while still being a good ghost story."

ISAAC YOUNG
Age 10, Shawnee, Kansas

"An educational tale in which Ms. Borin craftily weaves the perfect amount of both mystery and cleverness. I enjoyed it best when Noah confessed and opened up to the children. Out of all the books in this endearing series, this one is my favorite."

MIKAELA SAMSON
Age 12, Belton, MO

For photos and more information about the historical sites in The Ghost Adventures of Orion O'Brien, go to
www.orionkobrien.com